Aluta

ALUTA
Adwoa Badoe

Groundwood Books
House of Anansi Press
Toronto Berkeley

The author would like to acknowledge funding support from the Ontario Arts
Council, an agency of the government of Ontario.

Published in Canada and the USA in 2016 by Groundwood Books

Groundwood Books / House of Anansi Press
groundwoodbooks.com

We acknowledge for their financial support of our publishing program the Canada
Council for the Arts, the Ontario Arts Council and the Government of Canada.

Canada Council Conseil des Arts
for the Arts du Canada

ONTARIO ARTS COUNCIL
CONSEIL DES ARTS DE L'ONTARIO
an Ontario government agency
un organisme du gouvernement de l'Ontario

With the participation of the Government of Canada
Avec la participation du gouvernement du Canada | Canadä

Library and Archives Canada Cataloguing in Publication
Badoe, Adwoa, author
Aluta / Adwoa Badoe.
Issued in print and electronic formats.
ISBN 978-1-55498-816-7 (bound).—ISBN 978-1-55498-818-1
(html).—ISBN 978-1-55498-819-8 (mobi)
I. Title.
PS8553.A312A65 2016   jC813'.54   C2015-908441-5
C2015-908442-3

Jacket illustration by Shonagh Rae
Design by Michael Solomon

Printed and bound in Canada

MIX
Paper from
responsible sources
FSC® C016245

For my dad, Kankam Twum-Barima

Prologue
Thursday, July 22, 1982

Some things only happen in movies, I thought, as I sat on the wooden chair in a room with no windows and only one door. A naked pearl bulb hung from the ceiling and everything was painted white, as though nothing dirty could ever accumulate there.

I had been told to sit on the other side of the table, across from the thin man who had a tribal mark cut deep into one cheek. He had a thin pointy nose, high bulky forehead and beady eyes that never blinked.

His speech was slow and deliberate and he read his questions from a binder that lay open in front of him. I watched him as he wrote down everything I said.

"Your name?"

"Charlotte Adom."

"Full name?"

"Charlotte Abena Mampomaa Adom."

"Date of birth?"

"July 30th 1963."

Suddenly, I recalled that I had flipped the calendar just that morning. July 22, 1982. It was a Thursday morning.

"Father's name?"

"Joseph Manu Adom."

"Occupation?"

"Biology teacher, Achimota Secondary School."

"Mother's name?"

"Cecilia Esi Dansoa Adom. Teacher. Achimota Preparatory School."

"Siblings?"

"Sarah Adom."

"Where do you attend school?"

"University of Science and Technology."

"What degree are you taking?"

"BSc. Social sciences."

"Year?"

"First year."

The questions were easy, even if they were barked out by the man in the dark gray political suit who never smiled.

The questions continued.

"A Level?"

"Achimota School."

"O Level?"

"Achimota School."

"Are you on the university Student Representative Council?"

"Yes. I am the SRC secretary."

He wrote this down in his book. Then he closed the book, folded his hands together and placed them on the table. He fixed his gaze fully upon me.

Unease fluttered like bees in my belly. I was used to men staring, but not like this. A hostile, narrow squint instead of the usual look of charm or lasciviousness that

I encountered regularly as a young woman of marriage-
able age.

"Where were you going when you were apprehended
in the taxi?"

"I was going to visit my uncle."

"His name?"

"Mr. Kwadwo Owusu."

"Why would you visit him on a weekday morning?"

"He's retired."

Another silence as those small eyes bore into my soul. A
shiver passed through me but I didn't blink. It was important that I stayed steady and direct. I knew he was looking
for holes in my answers. He was looking to unnerve me.

"Why today? Why would you even be in Accra? Don't
you have exams coming up?"

"I have been studying hard. I needed a break to refresh,
and I needed a bit of money to finish the term," I replied.

"You are smart, Charlotte Adom. But I'm past playing
games. We have intelligence about a subversive NUGS
meeting in Accra. I believe you were on your way there."

"A NUGS meeting? I don't know about it," I said, glad
that I had not kept any record of the address that Banahene
had passed to me on a slip of paper. I had destroyed it earlier
that morning, after I had emptied my bag of everything
but my makeup and my wallet. I knew they would find
nothing on me when they took my bag away.

"Girl, you are in serious trouble. Treason is a serious
crime against the state. Don't think you're too young to
face a firing squad."

"I don't know anything," I said. But this time my voice
quavered.

11

"You know much, and you will tell all you know. Trust me." His voice was softer than ever but there was violence in his cold black eyes.

My gaze fell on the hand that tapped a pen against the table. His fingers were long and slender, his nails brownish and overgrown. Cruel hands.

"We are already aware of your meetings in a certain priest's house in Kumasi," he hissed.

"I don't know what you're talking about," I said.

To my surprise, he scraped his chair hard on the floor as he pushed himself away from the table. He picked up his binder and strode to the door. The door swung open and closed with a snug click, and I was left by myself.

Time passed, perhaps an hour. There was no clock in the room and they had taken my watch. I thought through the questions I had been asked. My answers were innocent enough and I hoped that I would soon be released. Then I could warn the others.

I walked cautiously to the door and tried it. It was locked. I returned to my chair and noted with unease that my bladder was filling.

I was anxious but not panicky. What would they gain by hurting a common student?

I thought about my last day with my boyfriend, Banahene. We had made love and I worried that I had sinned. I asked God for forgiveness. Surely the word was true that forgiveness was instant, at the point of confession. God would protect me.

The door opened and my interrogator was back. He offered me a glass of water but I declined, saying that I needed to urinate. I wasn't sure if the water was drugged.

So long as I wasn't dying of thirst, I'd stay away from any food or drink.

"You will hold your piss until I have the information I need," he said.

And for the first time he smiled, but his eyes were hard. That was when I felt the sweat wet my nose and armpits.

"Tell me about Banahene. Where is he? Where are they holding the meeting, and when does it start?"

I told him I didn't know where Banahene was.

"I barely know him except for SRC meetings," I said.

My interrogator opened a folder. He spread photographs on the table and told me to draw closer.

They were photos of Banahene and me walking side by side on campus. We were laughing at something and Banahene's hand rested on my waist.

"Now tell me about Banahene, you liar."

He moved fast, smacking my left cheek with his hand. I was more shocked than hurt, and a little pee escaped me. I tightened my groin and covered my face with my hand.

"Charlotte Adom, I am not here to play games. This is a matter of national security, and you are under a potential charge of treason. Do you understand?"

I struggled to hold back my tears.

"I just came to Accra to visit my parents. I was going to my uncle's house when I was brought here," I said.

Another slap landed on the other cheek and left me whimpering. I felt the warmth of my urine against the sides of my legs. The horror of it must have registered on my face.

Abruptly, my interrogator got up and left. And little by little I swallowed my sobs, but shame now covered me from head to toe.

Time passed. Three, four, five hours, maybe. I tried to talk to myself to hold up and not be intimidated. I told myself it was no shame to urinate when someone was holding you captive and beating on you.

I remembered something my dad used to say. "This too shall pass."

I was wet, uncomfortable and tired. A strange high-pitched sound pierced the air intermittently, as if metal was scraping on metal. It set me on edge.

The interrogator came back. He put a glass of water in front of me.

"Drink!" he said.

I drank the water but it did nothing to alleviate my anxiety, and soon my stomach began to cramp.

"Do you know Edmund Kwame Asare Bediako?"

"No, I don't know anyone by that name," I lied.

Why was he asking about Asare?

"Are you sure?"

"I'm sure."

"You are a member of the university's SRC?"

"Yes. I am the secretary," I said.

"What are you doing in Accra?"

"I'm visiting my parents," I said.

I wondered why he was repeating questions I had already answered.

"You are young, but being a student doesn't make you safe. I just want you to know you are being watched. We know you've been in certain meetings, in certain homes, talking to certain reactionaries. Your name has even come up with intelligence about coup plots. Be very careful. Next time we might not be so forgiving," he said.

14

I exhaled. Perhaps they would let me off soon. My stomachache had subsided but I began to feel woozy in my head. I must have nodded off.

Then I heard my name as if I was in a dream. My interrogator appeared to be shouting, yet his voice was distant. His questions were coming fast and I answered them. I could not help myself. I felt strange. I was suffocating. I wanted out of there. I wanted to stop talking about Banahene, the SRC, my parents and me.

I just wanted everything to stop.

1

I was sitting at the table in Room 803, reading, when my new roommate burst in through the door. She was followed by a trail of small-boys carrying everything from a small fridge to an apɔtɔyewa for crushing vegetables.

It was still very early days for me in residence at Africa Hall, and I didn't know what to think. I had waited five days for a roommate and suddenly there was Mary. She was in her third year and I knew she would not be looking forward to sharing a room with a first-year student.

Mary was pretty. Her mass of jheri curled hair bounced at every step. She had tiny feet and the smoothest round face. She carried along a whiff of delicate floral fragrance which I would later recognize as Anaïs Anaïs. Her eyebrows were picked into a thin line of surprise above her eyes, and spots of sweat burst through a thick layer of foundation. Even though she was petite, she was a little on the plump side — just like her personality.

Mary's voice was shrill as she picked on the small-boys, instructing them and chiding them all at once. She knew all of them by name.

"Hello," she trilled my way. "I'm Mary, and since I'm in third year, I should have the bottom bunk," she said.

We both stared at my yellow bedsheet tucked in around the mattress. My two pillows lay innocently at the head of the bed. I worked hard to stifle indignation as I yielded to years of inculcation in secondary school — seniority allowance! Then, it had always been best to comply with one's senior, but I wasn't sure if that applied in university.

My worst fears were coming true — a bossy roommate.

Mary had so many things. I watched as she unloaded a double-burner tabletop stove and set it up on the balcony table. She squeezed her fridge into the corner where the desk and the bookshelf met. Her covered bucket went beside mine on the balcony.

Then she unpacked her clothes and carefully arranged them in the closet.

I was very relieved when she didn't complain about using the lower shelves. That said she wasn't going to treat me as her junior in everything. Her alarm clock went on the shelf along with a set of pretty plates and glasses. Instead of plain bedsheets, she had beautifully patterned ones. She also had a soft baby-blue fleece blanket for a bedspread.

"Roomie, help me put up the curtains, please," she said.

I liked the familiar way in which she addressed me. I got off the chair and we put the prettiest lace curtain over our larger window at the back of the room. Then we stretched a blue curtain on the tall window at the front. She even had a curtain for the back door.

I had totally forgotten about curtains when I packed for school. So for the first week I was forced to use my spare bedsheet to cover my front window while I planned how to get curtains from home. Mary solved that problem, and I had to admit that it wasn't such a bad thing to get a senior for a roommate.

Then she played some reggae music on her JVC stereo radio-tape recorder, and I entered freshman heaven. Only fate could have made such a sophisticated roommate possible.

Later on, I'd learn that Mary was a Kumasi girl, with family right in town. She was in her third year of the three-year social sciences program. And she had a serious boyfriend — in fact a fiancé who had already performed the door-knocking rites of courtship.

For the first time since getting my A Level results, I felt lucky. In that first hour of meeting Mary, it was easier to believe that the University of Science and Technology was going to work out for me.

Here I was, six hours away from my home in Accra, and life was at last about to bud and blossom.

‹•›

My contribution to our household appliances in Room 803 was a heating coil. On the eighth floor we stored water in buckets overnight. This was because the pump could not push water up eight floors when all the bathrooms in our building were in use. Our showers became useless in the mornings. So we used the heating coil to warm our buckets of bath water after the night had chilled them to near freezing.

I woke up earlier than Mary for my African-child shower. That's what she called squatting in a shower stall and scooping bucket water with a small pail to wash soap-suds away. I could bathe with as little as half a bucket of water.

My heater was useful, but I didn't realize it was going to help me make friends with my neighbors in Room 802 — Juaben and Sylvia.

On Thursday, Juaben poked her head in my doorway and said, "Can I borrow your heating coil?"

Two tiny dimples appeared in her cheeks when she smiled. She was the kind of girl people would call black-beauty for her very dark chocolate skin. Afterwards, tall and slender Sylvia returned the heater. And by the next day we had established a routine around it.

I told them the history of our empty elevator shaft as we walked down the eight flights of stairs to the dining room. Mary said that it was boarded up because the builder had ordered a wrong-sized elevator when the building was brand new.

"That's more than fifteen years ago. They're never going to fix it," said Sylvia.

"No running water, no elevator. Eighth-floor problems," said Juaben with a sigh.

"First-year problems. We're going to spend all our money sending small-boys on errands. Poor Mary wasn't supposed to end up on the eighth floor," said Sylvia.

Mary never complained about having to put up with us

first-year students on the eighth floor. But she made jokes about the hours we spent matching our clothes and trying on makeup and different hairstyles.

She shunned the dining hall as if it was a place for beggars. But Sylvia, Juaben and I began every school day there. We didn't have rich boyfriends, and a breakfast of hot Hausa koko — corn porridge spiced with chili and sweetened with sugar — was the hearty base upon which to load our lectures for the day. After eating, we converged at the main entrance with other students for the twenty-minute walk to Mecca, where we had our lectures.

We talked about boys — the ones we fancied. We discussed campus parties. And as a faithful disciple of Mary, I showed Sylvia and Juaben how to pin their invites on the notice board in their room. At Tech there was a style of making miniature invitation cards, no bigger than a square inch and hand decorated with stars and glitter. Mary had taught me the pride of accumulating invitations all year long as proof of one's popularity.

I learned from Mary that it was best to go to parties with my girlfriends instead of going as the date of a guy who could cramp my style all night long. That way I could dance with whomever I wished. I shared this tidbit of wisdom with Juaben and Sylvia on one of those walks to Mecca.

Mary was a good roommate. But Sylvia and Juaben were my buddies — which meant that we took some lectures together, went to parties and even exchanged clothes.

And just like that, by the second week of term, my fear of not fitting in at university was gone. My future at Tech was looking good.

‹•›

Matriculation came two weeks into the term. Mary explained that it was a formal ceremony to welcome all first-year students to the university community. We were up early that Saturday with plenty of time to get ready for the event at the Great Hall. The eighth floor was never so busy. We were bumping into each other in the bathroom, on the balcony and in our doorways. Everyone was trying to look their finest.

Sylvia wore black pants and a striking red blouse. Juaben's straightened hair was pulled back along the sides and fluffed forward on the top in the popular look called Travolta. I wore my hair in a small afro and tucked a yellow rose just above my right ear. The rose matched the yellow flowers on my best blue dress. Funky brass bangles, large earrings and low-heeled black strappy sandals completed my look.

Then we were off to the Great Hall. I marveled at Juaben's courage on that long walk on her red high heels. She walked without missing a step.

The stairs on all sides of the Great Hall were crawling with first-year students. The boys were neatly dressed in long-sleeved shirts, ties and their best shoes. Only a few of them owned suits.

After all the fuss and makeup, there we sat, wilting like mountain flowers in the heat while speeches were made from the podium. With a neatly folded handkerchief, I dabbed at the sweat forming on my forehead while ceiling fans whirred uselessly above us. I was sorry for those professors who sat on the stage, arraigned in awkward black hats and pompous medieval gowns designed for temperate regions.

Afterwards photographers zigzagged among us. I joined the eighth-floor ladies in a group shot. I also posed with Sylvia and Juaben. Then I took some solo pictures to send home to my parents. There was a reason we dressed up so fine.

But as I approached Africa Hall with Sylvia and Juaben, I heard a splash and the sound of hoots and laughter.

Someone shouted, "Another one bites the dust!"

Mary had told me about the ponding ritual for first-year students. She had said it would be hard to escape the seniors who were hell bent on throwing us into the lobby fishpond while we were still in our best clothes. I could see them through the open door. There were perhaps fifteen of them.

I watched them chase some first-year students across the lobby. Whoever they caught, they swung by hands and feet like a pendulum, before dropping her into the pond.

It looked dangerous, and my greatest fear was swallowing a fish, or worse, algae. One had to be crazy to enjoy this kind of game.

I was wearing my best outfit. The label said it was 100 percent viscose and dry clean only. I wasn't going to let it into a dirty algae-ridden pond.

"What shall we do?" said Sylvia.

A girl who had just joined us said it was best to get it over and done with right away. But I was determined not to ruin my best dress. Juaben and Sylvia decided to go to town to visit Juaben's aunt until the evening, when things had died down. I didn't want to go with them. They took the path, stepping gingerly over loose stones. It was some distance to the junction. Those shoes would kill Juaben unless they found a taxi very quickly.

Soon they were out of sight. I crept forward with a bunch of fearful students until we were about sixty meters away from the hall entrance. I waited and watched until I understood the momentum of the ponding ritual. The crowd thinned as half an hour became an hour of waiting. There were more shouts and cheers. Then the excitement seemed to die down, as the ponders got tired of the ponding.

I took off my sandals and approached the entrance. They were about to pond someone. I slipped in quietly. As soon as I saw that they were all diverted, I dashed as fast as I could to the stairs of my block.

Just as I took the first few steps, I heard someone shout, "There goes Charlotte. Get her!"

But I was already up the first flight and taking the steps two at a time. They didn't bother to chase me because they already had a prey in hand. I heard their gleeful shouts as they threw another girl into the pond.

Panting, I continued up the stairs while my heartbeat sounded like sonic booms in my chest. By the time I reached the seventh floor, I was quite sure I would die.

Then, just as I stepped onto the eighth floor, I slammed into someone. We fell down together like bags of cement.

"You should watch where you're going," I said.

"Me?" he said incredulously. "You're telling me to watch?"

In the next moment we were both laughing.

"Sorry," I said. "I was escaping the ponding."

"Well, good luck. Although it's better to get it done now, and not when you're least expecting it."

"Not in this dress," I said.

"It is a pretty dress, but so are all the other dresses getting soaked right now."

"This is dry clean only," I said, dusting myself.

"Oh?"

Suddenly it occurred to me how silly it was to own a dry-clean-only dress in hot, dusty Kumasi.

He stuck out his hand. "I am Banahene. What's your name?"

"Charlotte. And I had better get to my room before they catch me and drag me down eight flights of stairs to drop me in a stinky pond."

"Charlotte? You're Mary's roommate. Mary is my cousin," he said.

"Mary hasn't mentioned any cousins."

"You think I'm lying. Come on, then. Mary can tell you herself."

Mary was cooking, and the aroma of her stew filled the air. She was surprised to see me with Banahene. She couldn't explain properly how they were related to each other. They shared an uncle in common, but the family tree was confusing with half-brothers, stepsisters and all.

Banahene was good company, and I guess he was hungry because he stayed until Mary's Jollof rice was ready. Mary dedicated the meal to my matriculation, and Banahene toasted me with our shared bottle of Coca-Cola.

"To Charlotte — wishing you a happy stay at the University of Science and Technology. If I were you, I'd take off that pretty, dry-clean-only dress and go back and let them throw me to the fish. It's better to get it over and done with now," he said, holding up his glass.

"Go and jump in the pond then," I said.

"Not after so great a meal," he replied with a twinkle in his eye.

That was how I met Banahene.

It was not my intention to fall in love with him.

2

I remember when I first met Mary's fiancé, William Opoku. Mary said to call him Willie. But Willie seemed too disrespectful for such a dignified man, and so I called him Mr. Opoku.

It was Saturday. I had just had a meal of fried plantains and beans at the dining hall. If there was anything I really loved, that was it. And I carried a plate upstairs for Mary. To tell the truth, I hoped she would decline the meal so I could have it later for dinner.

And there was Mr. Opoku in our solitary wooden armchair, looking shower-fresh in a burgundy golf shirt and black pants. Traces of his cologne hung in the air. I recognized him at once from the large framed photograph that stood in the corner of our worktable — Mary, with a hand on Mr. Opoku's chest, looking up at him with wonder in her eyes.

The most attractive thing about Mr. Opoku was the air of accomplishment that he exuded. He was confident and

collected — a complete man in control of his environ-
ment. And our tiny room felt out of place around him.

I observed Mary quietly as she fussed over her clothing. All Mary's clothing was fine. She could have worn
anything and she'd be the best dressed, but she had two
blouses picked out for the evening.

"Willie, this one, or that?" she asked, tilting her head
flirtatiously.

"Wear a dress tonight, baby — the blue one with the
straps and the slit at the side."

Even his voice was perfect. It was as if he knew everything Mary owned, and I was so impressed.

Mary pouted in a sexy kind of way. She wanted to wear
her black pedal pushers with a leopard pattern blouse or a
black-and-white shirt. Pedal pushers were in vogue.

She started to argue, but Mr. Opoku had a way with her.
Maybe it was because she so loved him. There were times
I wondered if he had some power over her. But Juaben said
love was a kind of power.

Mr. Opoku was a Kumasi lawyer — smart and tall for an
Ashanti man. He was from one of those families that everyone knew in the city. He had it all — a respectable career,
handsome face and a pretty girlfriend at the university.
Mr. Opoku spread his charm in softly spoken words, and
Mary knew she had got herself a real catch. When he
laughed, it was her eyes that lit up like stars.

"Why don't you join us this evening?" he said to me.

It took me a moment to understand that it was an invitation to go out with them. I placed the plantain and bean
dish carefully in the fridge and turned to face him.

"Where are you going?" I asked.

"Just out to dinner, and then some fancy dancing. Let's show you the Kumasi lights." A hint of humor brightened his eyes and gave way to infectious laughter.

Still, I looked to Mary for direction. I certainly did not want to crash her evening. I'd heard that insensitive roommates who crashed every visit and every date were the worst of afflictions in residence.

So when Mary said, "Great idea," I gladly said yes.

Mr. Opoku was too important to be asked to wait outside like an ordinary undergrad while I changed. So I took my clothes next door to 802, where Juaben and Sylvia helped me to look my best. We agreed that Mary was bound to outclass me with her designer couture from England. My aim was just to keep up. I didn't want to be the country mouse to her town mouse.

In the end, I wore my dark brown corduroy trousers and a sparkly yellow shirt. Sylvia made up my face with blue eye pencil and eye shadow. My lips were painted full red and outlined in black. Juaben lent me her black evening bag and shoes to match.

And there was Mary, stunning in her blue strappy dress and tall stiletto heels.

Mr. Opoku said that he was the lucky one, because he had two of Africa Hall's most beautiful ladies with him for the evening. I let his flattery linger over me.

In Mr. Opoku's Mercedes-Benz, S-class, cool air wafted over me. The olive-green masterpiece had black leather seats and tinted glass.

As we zoomed off to the muffled sound of the powerful

car, nobody would have known I had come to school with two old suitcases and a small cardboard box of canned fish and evaporated milk.

‹•›

At first we went to City Hotel. It had seen better days, and the air conditioner grumbled loudly without cooling the air. Still, the food was tasty, and everything washed down very well with the coldest glass of Star beer. Mr. Opoku and Mary enjoyed Jollof rice with grilled chicken and garden salad, drenched with Heinz salad cream. I had ordered my all-time eat-out favorite — a club sandwich.

I cut cautiously through layers of toast, chicken, bacon and tomato, hoping I would not drip mayonnaise on everything. Once I took my first bite, I no longer noticed the businessmen huddled around their dinner tables talking loudly. Neither did I care about the flickering ceiling lights or the missing tiles on the wall or the chairs worn out by use.

I became bold and asked if we might go to Hedonist, the only nightclub I'd heard about in Kumasi.

"Hedonist has great music, but varsity students ruin it for everyone," Mr. Opoku said.

"How come?" I asked. Everyone said Hedonist was the place to go when there were no parties on campus.

"They're just loud and rowdy — like children," he replied.

"They can't handle their drinks," Mary said with a chuckle.

"Nkɔdaa-nkɔdaa, little children," said Mr. Opoku, as he set his glass on a cardboard coaster.

"I hope you won't think I'm childish, too," I said.

My sarcasm was lost on Mr. Opoku.

"It's the boys who behave childishly," he said.

‹•›

So we drove to a nightclub at Nhyiaeso, and the car park was jam-packed. Even from outside, the music did violence to the night. There were several groups of people loitering outside smoking, and their curious eyes followed us through the arched entrance. I wondered if Mary knew that it was my first night out to a club.

"Wee smokers," Mary whispered into my ear. And I recognized the pungent smell of marijuana smoke.

Inside, we were hailed with loud calls from one of the garden tables. Mr. Opoku was obviously well known here, and his friends were like him — quite a bit older, well-to-do Kumasi professionals. We settled among them.

One thing was clear. These men had money to spend, and their laughter filled the air all around us.

Then I understood what Mary meant about childish undergrads. She was comfortable among Mr. Opoku's friends, and she chatted away happily with both men and women. She laughed as loudly as any one of them.

I danced with one man, and then another. And I noticed that even those men who were sitting next to their partners cast curious glances at me.

I was more than a little intrigued. These people had their own jokes. They expressed their worth in large gold watches, shiny black shirts and blood-red Italian leather shoes. They mixed English and Twi easily. Almost every one of the men flashed a large gold signet ring. I was reminded that Ashanti was the land of gold.

And in this way Mary introduced me to Kumasi city night life and its businessmen.

I was curious about the women at our table. Mary seemed to be well acquainted with two of them. But the third one seemed out of place. She wore a white dress with shoulder pads and big sleeves. She said little all evening, punctuating every two-word response with a please. Please yes. Please no. She seemed obsessed with a plate of chicken wings, which she picked at gingerly, almost as if she expected a fried wing to come alive and fly off the plate. She sipped cautiously at her glass of beer.

Mary must have noticed me watching the girl in white, because she leaned over and whispered, "She's just a small-girl, probably from one of the secondary schools around. I don't know what she's doing here. She is way out of her league."

That was how I felt, too, but I was not going to admit it. So I added my opinions to the conversations at the table and tried to exude confidence.

The band should have stuck to highlife music. Instead it vacillated between good highlife and weak renditions of pop and disco, played with highlife guitar styling. I got up to dance with a man whose big teeth flashed white and strong. He was a short man and very jolly. He made a joke and we laughed together. Every now and then he pulled a white handkerchief out of his pocket and mopped furiously at his forehead. It was impossible not to sweat on the packed dance floor.

I had just returned to my seat when I heard, "Dance with me."

I turned around. It was the man who sometimes spoke with an American accent. He had kept up a humorous commentary all evening, spicing his jokes with occasional profanity.

Asare was stocky and well built. He was very dark skinned, and he held his shoulders back and his forehead high. I might have described him as arrogant, except for the smile that played around his lips.

I never asked, but I think the girl in white was his date.

"Come on, Charlotte, I like Kool and the Gang," he insisted.

We danced to "Get Down On It." I liked Asare's moves and so I didn't hold back. Then the DJ played Roberta Flack's "Killing Me Softly," and Asare drew me easily into his arms.

"Where are you from?" he asked, speaking slightly above my ear.

I leaned into him to say, "Accra!"

"Do you live in Accra, or do you come from Accra?"

"I come from Kibi, Eastern Region."

"Ei! Kibi women are beautiful but cantankerous," he said into my ear.

"I don't think so."

"You're beautiful but maybe not cantankerous, then."

"Neither," I replied.

"Yes, you are beautiful." And his breath was warm and moist around my ear. It disturbed me a little — an awkwardness in my belly. I said nothing until at last the song ended.

"You should dance with your date," I said as I wriggled out of his arms. I'd had enough of older men for one night.

⟨•⟩

I was taking courses in political science, history and English. I wasn't sure yet which of the three would become my major. I didn't care about politics. I had chosen political science because I expected it to be easier than economics or law. At Tech there was this idea that political science was a course of only medium difficulty, so I hoped to do well at it.

It was at my political science course that I first met Dr. Ampem. And it was in his class that I met Jordan on the morning of the first Dawn Broadcast.

I was fast asleep, dreaming about my hair — long and straight, blowing in the breeze. Mary had promised to relax my hair. She said I had to choose between a natural downcut or straightened hair, because big poufy afros were out of fashion.

From far off, a song filtered through my sleep and wove itself like a colorful thread into the pattern of my dream.

A voice spoke urgently in the pre-dawn darkness, "Repent, and be saved!"

Which impassioned Africa Hall sister could be so bold as to shout down our dawn dreams on a Friday? I climbed down the ladder to find Mary on the lower bunk, valiantly holding onto her sleep, her head buried beneath the pillow.

As quietly as I could, I opened the door to the front balcony and stepped up against the balustrade to find a bunch of girls huddled on the low roof of the porter's lodge, singing.

As the first rays of dawn entered the darkness, I could make the ladies out in their dressing-gowns. The leader brought the song to a close with the sinners' prayer.

Thanks to them, nobody would be late for a 7 a.m. lecture.

The piping hot Hausa koko changed my sour mood for the better, and I joined my favorite group of girls for the walk to Mecca. The mild sun meant no sweat or stickiness. And the gentle breeze stirred up fallen leaves and blew them ahead of us.

"I swear, I thought Judgment Day had come upon us suddenly, like a thief in the night," Sylvia said. "I startled right up and couldn't sleep again. In fact, I checked to make sure Juaben was still in bed and not raptured." She raised her hands to the sky.

We all burst out laughing. Sylvia could be so dramatic.

"The girls can preach, eh? I repented right there on my bed," Juaben admitted. "I need a message like that from time to time, to remind me that life is not all about boys and clothes."

"You mean books and degrees," said Sylvia.

We often talked about those things — boys, degrees, marriage, careers and, occasionally, living to make a difference. Sylvia was all about fun. Juaben wanted a man like Mr. Opoku and an early marriage right after school.

I was never sure exactly what I wanted. I guess I wanted to be popular, and beautiful, and smart, and in love.

"Let's resolve to serve the Lord better. As a junior in secondary school, I was in the Scripture Union Club," said Juaben.

"I used to be the president of the Catholic Students Association but I think sleeping during the hours of darkness has to be a fundamental human right. I hope they don't preach us awake every week," I said, gathering some courage to speak my mind.

"Charlotte the lawyer," Sylvia chuckled.

"I didn't know you were Catholic. You don't even have a rosary," said Juaben.

I thought about the black velvety pouch in which I kept my Book of Prayers and my rosary.

"I'm just lazy about saying my prayers," I replied.

Books, degrees, clothes, boys and now religion. Everything was competing for our attention.

3

I was among the first to arrive at the lecture hall for political science. I squeezed into a chair in the front row — the kind with a writing board attached to one arm. Then I settled down to wait for Dr. Ampem.

He came in close to the hour and took some time to arrange his papers on the table.

He looked up, caught my eyes and smiled.

"How are you today, Charlotte?"

"Fine, sir." I was surprised that he knew my name.

In the next five minutes, the class filled up quickly. Dr. Ampem was one of those lecturers who always started on time. A very smooth speaker, he delivered his talks powerfully and fast. And his face was animated behind small black round spectacles.

I was an avid note-taker and I was torn between keeping my eyes on my notebook and watching his gestures and expressions.

We were studying the politics of the 1950s. I had studied much about the colonial history of Ghana in secondary school. I knew that our country had been called the Gold Coast. It had been ruled by the British as a colony from 1902 to 1957, when our people had demanded their independence. We always made much of Independence Day and Dr. Kwame Nkrumah, our first president. As Ghanaians we held on to the pride of being the first of the colonized countries of Africa to win our independence. For this reason, Nkrumah was a great hero, but his legacy had ended in shambles when his government was overthrown in a coup d'état in 1966. My father thought of that coup as deliverance from Nkrumah's growing tyranny. But there were others like Dr. Ampem who blamed all of Ghana's current problems on that coup.

Dr. Ampem had a passion for the late Dr. Nkrumah and his grand plans for Ghana and Africa. He would pause from time to time during a lecture to deride several heads of state for running down Nkrumah's legacy.

Someone made a comment that Dr. Limann and the People's National Party had returned the nation to Nkrumah's socialist ideology.

"Pretenders," said Dr. Ampem with a snort. "This current government is weak. And there is no change without societal grassroots involvement. That is more important than those prayer meetings people attend so vigorously on this campus."

"This morning I heard my first Dawn Broadcast," I said.

"Tell us about it," he said.

"I woke up to the sound of women singing in the

darkness. They were shouting from the porter's rooftop about salvation in Jesus Christ."

Several other girls had heard it, too. Soon the discussion transitioned into opinions on human rights, religious rights and common nuisance laws. I realized for the first time that there were some Muslim men in my class.

"If we're to insist on nuisance laws, then what about those night-long Saturday parties held at many halls?"

I turned around to look at the speaker. He was a lanky young man wearing a starched white shirt, simple black trousers and sandals one might buy at Makola market.

He looked like someone who might give a Dawn Broadcast someday.

"Can you tell us your name when you rise to speak?" said Dr. Ampem.

So the young man told us his name — Jordan Braimah. And I gave mine.

"Our Saturday jams are too much fun to give up. So I guess I'll just have to give up my morning sleep to allow the lax state of nuisance laws to persist," I said.

The class applauded.

"Good one, Charlotte," said Dr. Ampem.

"We are generally a loud people. For generations we have been awakened by traditional drums on traditional rites days, and also by the Muslim prayer call in the Zongos at dawn," said Jordan mildly.

"Don't forget the church bells calling the Catholics to mass," said Dr. Ampem.

Jordan laughed. He had won the argument, and Dr. Ampem picked up the thread of his lecture once more.

Dr. Ampem revealed that Nkrumah had cut his political teeth during his student days in America where he organized the African Students Association of America and Canada, and became its president.

"Many more of you should become interested in the Student Representative Council and the National Union of Ghana Students, here on campus," said Dr. Ampem. "If you're going to be great, it starts right here in college. There's no better way to understand politics than to engage with it. When I look around, more often than not I see medical students and architects in student political positions. I ask myself, *Where are my students?* Show me by hands those of you who might consider student politics?"

Three hands went up. They were all males. One of them was Jordan.

"What about my ladies?" Dr. Ampem looked around and settled on me. "What about you, Charlotte?"

"I don't know, sir."

"What's there to know?" he demanded.

Thankfully the hour was up, and people were already gathering their books. I pushed my chair back against the hard concrete floor.

"We'll talk about it next time," said Dr. Ampem, looking directly at me.

I couldn't very well say politics was not my thing. I was a student of political science, after all.

‹•›

I loved the weekends. I would sleep in two extra hours to make it to breakfast by nine. In Africa Hall our mornings were marked by the shrill shouting of women from one block to the other, as friends conducted conversations by bush telephone. I would rest my arms on the balustrade in front of 803 and talk across to Emily, a schoolmate from Accra. It was our way of catching up on each other. Nobody wanted to walk down and up eight floors.

Jonas, my small-boy, would run errands for me. Nimble small-boys made quite a bit of money as Africa Hall ladies sent them back and forth on errands.

First, I would send Jonas to buy some tomatoes, eggs and a can of mackerel from the small market in a corner of our car park. Then I would engage him to do my laundry.

I thought he had a special affinity for me, but Mary was skeptical.

"Don't get taken in by that rascal. He treats everybody the same way," she said, warning me not to tip too much.

Mary always preferred to hire one of the cleaners to do her laundry. But adult cleaners were more expensive, and they turned their noses up at first-year students.

Mary chose a Saturday to relax my hair for the first time. Jonas had just finished doing my laundry on the balcony, and I got him to fetch extra buckets of water. I had bought my hair relaxer kit in town on Mary's advice, and I trusted her utterly, even though I knew my mother would disapprove.

Mary had urged me to relax my hair. She said there were so many more ways to style longer hair than I could ever dream with my natural hair. So I sat quietly on the chair as she parted lines in my thick springy hair. She smeared my scalp with dabs of Vaseline petroleum jelly. Then she carefully spread the barrier jelly right around my hairline and over my ears to prevent any burns.

She told me that the worst thing that could happen was getting relaxer cream in my eyes.

"When I get to the front, just close your eyes, Charlotte."

She opened the jar of Ultra Sheen Relaxer and began to apply the chemical with the handle of a comb. She was quick, and all I had to do was hold the two ends of the towel together at my neck.

She began to work my hair in little tufts, and the strong scent of lye stung my nostrils.

"You can open your eyes, roomie," she said. Whenever she called me roomie, I felt especially close to her.

I stared at myself in the mirror. My entire head was covered with white cream.

"When shall we wash it out?" I asked.

"We should let it stay on as long as possible because your hair is coarse virgin growth. But if your scalp begins to burn, we shall wash it off at once. Don't worry," she said.

Jonas had fetched six buckets of water to rinse out the lye, shampoo and conditioner in their turn. Mary organized the hair-washing process in the bathroom. I sat and waited until she came back.

I began to feel some spots on the back of my head stinging, and I told Mary.

She checked the clock. "Wait a while longer."

I tried to focus on other things — a timetable on our notice board, three party invites stuck next to each other, the photograph of Mary and Mr. Opoku on the table, and even the detail on our curtain fabric.

But the stinging got worse, attacking me all over my head.

"Mary, that's it. I am on fire!" I said.

"Okay, let's go to the bathroom," she said.

I was so grateful for the coolness of the water on my head, as she carefully washed the lye out. Mary neutralized the alkali with a special shampoo. Then she conditioned my hair, rinsed it and patted it with a towel. She took me back to our room and sat me in front of the desk.

I stared at myself in the mirror. My hair felt strange on my scalp, tangled up like a miserable mop, and longer than I'd ever seen it.

What was it about long hair that made us submit to harsh chemical treatment? My mother believed only in natural hair, never having used the pressing comb even when it was popular in her day.

"Length softens a face and adds a touch of mystery," said Mary, as she combed through my hair gently. Then, parting small bits at a time, she inserted pink rollers. Afterwards, she fished a hand-held dryer from one of her drawers and plugged it in.

It roared to life and she said, "This will take forever, Charlotte, because we don't have a real salon dryer."

I was impressed. How did Mary know these things?

"If you couldn't do anything else in this world, you could run a hair salon, Mary. You are amazing," I said.

We talked above the roar of the dryer, and I told her how mad my dad would be at my straightened hair.

"Too bad for him. You're a big girl now, and you have your own bangla money to spend," said Mary.

"Getting a government allowance is the best thing about university," I said.

I told Mary about my dad, Mama and my younger sister, Sarah. I had lived my entire life in a bungalow on the grounds of a boarding school because my father was a secondary school biology teacher.

While I was in secondary school, I spent full weeks of long vacation indoors reading. I could not get enough of Sidney Sheldon books — thrillers with strong and beautiful female characters, which I borrowed from my cousins.

And Mama would complain that I'd changed.

"Why do you brood so, Charlotte?" she would say. "You used to play all day with the neighborhood children. You were always going to one birthday party or another."

What could I say? It all began in Form One in Achimota Secondary School, where Dad taught. At age twelve, I had been as excited as anyone else to head off to boarding school. I was particularly thrilled to get into Achimota. All my life, I had seen students pass back and forth along the pathways of the school, and I couldn't wait to be one of them. I wanted to escape my home and my parents' tyranny to reside with other girls. I wanted to experience those adventures I had read about in Enid Blyton's Malory Towers series.

But it took only the briefest of introductions to Slessor House for me to realize that first formers were the scum of the earth. We were sent about on endless errands and made to entertain all seniors at their whim, day or night, whenever we were not at class.

I was picked on doubly. I discovered too late that my dad had a reputation for harsh punishment, and I became the scapegoat for his crimes.

Dad gave difficult biology tests and was much disliked for his rampant use of detentions. The students had given him the name Tension, which they tried to pass on to me. For seven years I tried not to let his reputation rub off on me. I could only look ahead to university to experience total liberty.

Once I settled into Tech, I began to realize the advantage of distance. It would take very lovey-dovey parents to drive the five to seven hours from Accra just to visit. It would also take a lot for news of my activities to travel from Kumasi.

With each day that I lived on campus, I seemed to grow a little larger in my heart and a little freer from restrictions. I was ready to turn into that cool, smart person who lived life with panache. And so I was happy to sacrifice one week's feeding allowance to buy the hair-relaxer kit. I guess I was hoping that Mary's regularly missed meals at the dining hall would be enough to feed me for that week.

‹•›

My new hairdo transformed me totally, and it was hard for even me to take my eyes off the image in the mirror. Fresh and floppy, I gave my loose curls some additional bounce by passing my fingers through them, fluffing them up.

That night we had a party to go to at Queen's Hall. I couldn't wait to show off my new look. I loved my sleek Huggers jeans with the golden zippers on every pocket — a gift from my cousin when she traveled to England. Silver glitter outlined my back pockets. I tucked in my white body-hugging shirt and borrowed Mary's belt, which had a fancy buckle. I exchanged necklaces with Sylvia. There was so much activity between our eighth-floor rooms as we primped and fussed, helping one another to dress just right.

Juaben shared her makeup with a bunch of us — eye shadow, mascara, lipstick and blush. We sprayed perfume, one on another. There was much giggling. Then, close to midnight, we left the hall, a bevy of females dressed to kill.

From his desk, Porter Afriyie watched us with judgment in his eyes.

"We'll be back soon, Mr. Afriyie," I said.

"The hall will be closed *very* soon," he replied.

We didn't care. No cool chick went to parties earlier than midnight.

‹•›

How we danced that night! We danced to hot pop, and we swayed to slow music. We danced to the Commodores, Michael Jackson and Barry White.

I fooled around with my girlfriends on the dance floor, doing crazy new steps from Accra. There were wild cheers, down-low movements and swirling hip circles. There were screams of delight as we danced to the groove.

I did not believe it could get any better.

After that party, traffic to our floor increased threefold. Mary said the October Rush had begun. So many boys wanted to be friends with us. Sometimes I had to escape to the library to finish off my class projects and assignments.

I knew my parents. There would be absolutely no grace for me if I showed up at home with poor grades.

4

Asare — with his dramatic American accent — was one of those who chased me relentlessly after I straightened my hair. I marveled at how he could use the word fuck like a sort of garnish on his frustrations.

Mary coerced me into another group date, saying Asare had harassed Mr. Opoku into arranging it.

The truth was that Asare wasn't bad looking. He had beautiful skin, a hawkish nose and a wicked grin. There was something high in his look— royal genes, possibly. He seemed well aware of his charms, but it was a poor choice to drip a pretentious American accent all over his speech.

"I feel yuh, babe. A-betcha. You gonna do righ' by me, mehn?" he would say, stretching out his vowels endlessly. His compliments after a pint or two of beer were outrageously overdone. *Shiee!*

We sat outdoors to escape the thick cigarette smoke. Outdoors was also easier for talking while loudspeakers blasted music in the dance hall.

We had returned to that same club at Nhyiaeso. Mary and Mr. Opoku had gone inside to dance, and I suspected that they were trying to give us some privacy.

Asare turned to me. "Babe, you know I admire an intelligent woman. Just looks and boobs ain't enough. I'm looking for more lasting treasure." He tapped at his temple with one finger.

I could have laughed, but I held it back. "I would have thought that more lasting treasure lies in the heart."

"See, you're smart, babe! That's what I'm getting at."

"This baby's got teeth, Asare, and she's watching you," I said, wagging my finger in his face.

Asare chuckled, took my hand in his and kissed it.

I had to admire his tenacity. I ordered a plate of chicken and fries and declined the Gulder beer he offered.

Suddenly, I remembered the timid girl in white, and her plate of chicken. For a moment I tensed up, until I realized I was up to this. I wasn't sixteen. I was in university, a member of a small cohort of the nation's best-educated women.

I pulled my hand out of his and he made a sad face.

The name of the disco was so apt. The Fox Trap. I wondered how long Mr. Opoku and Mary would last inside, where the air conditioners competed in vain against the Kumasi humidity, cigarette smoke and the hot sweaty bodies.

They didn't last very long. I looked up, and there they were at our table, already saying goodbye. They had another party to attend.

"Asare's a good guy, Charlotte. He will take care of you and drop you safely at Africa Hall. I trust him," said Mr. Opoku.

To be honest, I felt a little stranded, but I had to trust Asare. Even more, I had to trust me. So I stuck with Coca-Cola and Muscatella, while Asare drank more beer. We talked and danced.

Then at about ten-thirty, I asked to be dropped back at Africa Hall.

"Why so early?" asked Asare.

"I have a group discussion," I lied. I wanted to get back before the porters locked the hall at midnight. But it wasn't just that. Leaving early was one way of making sure my driver was not too drunk. And the group-work excuse was perfect for saying our goodbyes at the car.

I knew Mary was likely not spending the night at the hall, and I didn't want Asare to come upstairs with me.

‹•›

Asare's BMW was black, and the windows were a very dark tint. It made you curious as to who was inside, and why they had such a desire for privacy. Asare called it The Witch.

It was a different world inside the car. A low-slung bucket seat cradled me like a baby. Dashboard lights winked suggestively, and even the potholes were subdued before us.

It was almost with reluctance that I got out of the car at Africa Hall. I watched as Asare primed his engine and roared off like a teenager showing off his rich dad's car. I waved, although it was impossible to see if he waved back.

It was hard not to like the relaxed company of accomplished men who could wine and dine you outside the limitations of a weekly allowance. Yet Sylvia had made good arguments for the fun and freedom we had with our university guys. Older guys demanded more from their girlfriends.

I was startled by strong hands gripping my shoulders hard from behind.

"Aha! Now we have you," I heard someone say.

It was Alice Donkor, the leader of the notorious ponders.

"Nobody gets away from the pond initiation. It is part and parcel of being an Africa Hall lady. We'll give you double for outsmarting us the first time," she threatened.

I could have kicked myself for losing my guard so completely. I didn't say another word as unsympathetic laughter surrounded me. I knew there was nothing for it. Six girls pushed and dragged me to the pond. They didn't even let me take off my shoes. They grabbed my arms and legs, swung me twice and dropped me into the pool with a shout.

"Pom-pom-pom. Another one bites the dust!"

I rose to the surface, sputtering. To my disgust, I had swallowed pond water. I clawed my way out of the pond and algae, thankful that my shoes had stayed on my feet. Otherwise I would have left them in the pond.

I spat out saliva with my anger. Best not to react to these foolish girls, I thought. They would easily pond me again.

I found my way to the stairs, avoiding the porter's eyes. My dress clung in all the wrong places.

I was beyond mad.

Like an apparition, Banahene appeared at the foot of the stairs.

"Charlotte," he called softly.

I ignored him and climbed up the first flight of stairs, dripping my shame on every step. It wasn't just that I was wet and miserable, but the thought that he'd been right and that they'd had the last laugh was too much.

Suddenly tears pushed past my eyelids. Everything was wet now, even my eyes.

I stomped up all one hundred stairs before I realized that I had left my bag beside the pond. My keys were in my bag, the door was locked, and Mary was out with Mr. Opoku. It would be nearly impossible to find small-boys around at that time of night.

Still, I was about to shout for one, when Banahene rounded the last flight of stairs.

"I realized you left this behind," he said with too straight a face.

"Thank you," I murmured, taking the bag from him.

"No worries," he said. Then, as he walked off, he added, "It happens to everyone. Just laugh it off and have a shower. Nobody will remember tomorrow."

"Liar," I said to his retreating back. "You will always remember."

He turned and smiled.

"You're right. I will always remember."

‹•›

I thought I could never be friends with Banahene again, but I was wrong. The next night he came to visit, and he brought me a Mars bar.

"A peace offering," he said, handing it to me.

"Where did you get that?" I asked. A long time ago my uncle had taken my sister and me to the diplomatic shop in Accra and bought us Mars bars.

"My dad brought a box of these from his last trip to England. I was saving the last one for a special day," said Banahene.

"Thank you," I said.

"Aren't you going to eat it?"

"Not now. I'm going to save it for a very special moment."

"Come on, Charlotte. It's a peace offering. It's meant to be shared."

And so I peeled off the wrapper, took a bite and held it to his lips.

"Just a tiny piece," I said. Then we both began to laugh.

That was the night Banahene took me to the SRC meeting. He said he wanted to show me that there was more to life than parties, ponds and nightclubs.

So we walked to Independence Hall where the Student Representative Council meeting was being held. It was loud — boys shouting each other down and arguing about student loans and allowances. Still, I listened and observed, because Dr. Ampem had made a point of telling our class to engage with student politics.

There was one very colorful individual called Mensah, who kept shouting to intimidate the others.

"I have the floor!" he shouted, and his face was tight with anger. "I don't know which of you can stretch that small amount of money to accommodate three meals in modern Ghana. Maybe some of you are bangla magicians but I am not. They are starving us. And they won't take our protests seriously unless we demonstrate. Let's teach them that a hungry man is an angry man."

He really was angry as he stood there in a green T-shirt boasting the face of Che Guevara. There were fewer than twenty people representing the entire student body, and only two other women besides me. Mensah tried to get a motion on the floor but he could find nobody to second it.

Banahene whispered to me, "Mensah always complains about bangla. That's why nobody has any more patience for him. It is the same story every day. Some of us call him Bangla Mensah."

"Why is our food allowance called bangla?" I asked.

Banahene explained that it had something to do with United Nations Food Aid that Bangladesh had received in a time of crisis. Students made fun of everything.

I was surprised at how rowdy it was. Not boring as Mary had said. No wonder women stayed away. Still, I perked up at a discussion of student loans. The SRC president was hopeful of an increase in the loan amount, as they had been in talks with the government. Someone said that no amount of money could make up for inflation.

"The cedi is a useless thing now. Once upon a time students traveled chartered flights to England on those loans," he said.

On the walk back, Banahene told me a little more about each of the SRC officers. The president was in the School of Medical Sciences and the secretary was in architecture-design. The treasurer was a student of planning.

Dr. Ampem was right. There were no political science students among the executives.

"It's not just political science students who don't care about the SRC. Most students feel they have better things to do than come for a meeting," said Banahene.

"I'm going to keep coming. At the very least, I may learn to argue down boisterous guys."

"Go girl! Maybe you'll be my aide-de-camp when I stand for SRC president," he said.

"Really?" I said.

"I'll only stand if I think I can win. I don't like losing," he said with a chuckle.

"Nobody likes to lose."

"Some of us are really bad losers, though," Banahene replied. And by the crooked smile on his face, I knew he had remembered my ponding.

"Nasty boy," I said.

"You know I am your everlasting fan," he said.

‹•›

The term rushed on as if on wheels. There were quizzes and projects, sports activities and gospel concerts, but there were also parties. Banahene and I attended SRC meetings whenever they were called.

Banahene always visited us in Room 803, so I was surprised one evening when he suggested that I go with him to see his hall.

"Let me show you the greatest hall of all," he said. "Then we can go and buy kelewele."

The promise of kelewele hooked me, but I also wondered how different the men's hall would be from ours.

As we passed by the porter's lodge I glanced at my pigeon hole. There was an envelope in it. I wedged the tip of my finger into the corner of the envelope and teased it open to find a folded note.

It read quite simply, *Let's meet tomorrow at 7 p.m. at the faculty. Ampem.*

"Banahene, look at this. The only Ampem I know is my lecturer. Why is he asking me to meet him at Mecca?"

"You are learning," said Banahene wryly.

"Learning what?"

"About life."

"What does he want?" I asked.

"Maybe you'll know when you see him."

"I'm not going," I said. "This could even be one of my course mates impersonating him."

"It could be a trick, but I doubt it," said Banahene.

"I'll see him in class, and if he mentions it, then I'll ask what he wants."

"Okay."

"Aren't you going to give me any advice?"

"No. You're a big girl," said Banahene.

‹•›

Outside Republic Hall, where Banahene resided, a bunch of guys were passing a soccer ball around. Inside, a weight-lifting competition was going on and Banahene joined in with loud cheers for his friends.

Banahene was a guy's guy, boisterous and full of fun. It was a side of him I had never seen. He introduced me around and before long I was chatting with the guys. Later on, when the champion weightlifter had been named, we left the verandah for his room.

"Your single room is bigger than mine," I said in disbelief.

"This building is older than yours. In Ghana, things regress over the years and the same amount of money buys less space."

"There is no equity in this arrangement," I said jealously.

There were several hockey sticks leaning against the balcony wall, and a basketball resting in the corner.

"Do you play a lot of sports?" I asked.

"Half my life is spent at Paa Joe Stadium."

"And you still have time to visit Africa Hall?" I teased.

"I am a sharp-brain when it comes to my studies," he replied.

"I wish I was really good at sports," I said, grabbing a hockey stick.

"You don't have to be a star. Play for fun and exercise. I'll be coaching women's hockey this term," he said.

I liked Banahene. I was impressed by his interest in a broad range of things. He seemed to have more of a balance than I had noticed in my girlfriends in Africa Hall.

I decided I would try more things at Tech.

5

I thought about the note while Dr. Ampem was teaching, but there was nothing odd in his manner throughout the lecture. He didn't avoid me and neither did he fixate on me.

It had to be a course mate's prank.

The class ended, and I was focused on fitting all my books into my bag. When I looked up again, Dr. Ampem was hovering over me with a roguish grin on his face. My heart sank.

"Charlotte, did you get my note?" he asked.

"I got the note, sir, but I thought someone was impersonating you."

"It wasn't a prank," he said.

And I was at a loss for words.

Dr. Ampem was good looking in a careless way. He had a tired goatee and a thick untamed afro. He reminded me of the Nigerian novelist, Wole Soyinka — brilliant and handsome. His best features were his bright eyes which crinkled easily with humor. Laughing eyes.

"Well, Charlotte, can you meet me tonight at seven o'clock in my office?"

"Sir?"

"Well?"

"Okay, sir."

Surely Dr. Ampem was not going to hit on me! For the first time, I regretted relaxing my hair. Perhaps I looked more mature than my age.

At dinner that night, we ate together village style in Room 803 — Sylvia, Juaben, Mary and me.

I dipped my right hand into the deeper bowl, made a small ball of gari with my fingertips. The other bowl contained shitor — spicy fried pepper — and corned beef.

We ate fast, tongues on fire and hands brushing each other's impatiently. I told them about Dr. Ampem.

"Don't go," said Mary.

"I have to. He's my lecturer and I don't want to spend the rest of the semester playing cat and mouse with him," I said.

"You'll make things worse by having a confrontation. This man isn't just anybody, and he can make you fail your exams," she said.

"If he can make me fail for confronting him, then he can make me fail if I don't show up. I have to get to the bottom of things."

"I'll go with you. He won't be able to say or do much if there is a witness," said Sylvia.

"That's a great idea," I said, relieved. "Thank you."

Juaben wanted to go, too. But I thought one more person would be too much.

"With just Sylvia, I can say that walking to Mecca after

dark frightens me. Let's beat him at his own game," I said happily.

‹•›

My slippers tapped hard against the soles of my feet, as we walked the paved road to Mecca. It was too dark for short-cuts. Sylvia was wiser, for she had put on a pair of canvas shoes and socks, which covered her feet completely — just in case there was a snake or scorpion hiding in the brush.

It was a warm night and quite bright, with a full moon hovering low in the sky. The pitter-patter of my heart was about defiance. Dr. Ampem had made his move and I had countered it by taking a witness. I remembered my mother upbraiding me for being too competitive, and not allowing my sister and cousins to win at Monopoly or Scrabble.

"They're so much younger than you, Charlotte," she would say, but it had never mattered one bit to me.

I loved it best when I beat my father at a board game. Then I showed him no mercy for all that I suffered in school because of him.

Dad, who was a poor loser, once said, "I wish you would use this same aggression to get good grades in school, instead of the mediocrity you have shown at important exams."

That comment made my victory against Dad sweeter than ever. It would feel good to win against Dr. Ampem, too.

Soon enough, Sylvia and I arrived at the social sciences building. Our faculty was in a four-story building at the very end of Mecca.

I stopped at the bottom of the stairs. My breathing was fast and shallow. We climbed up to the second floor and I held my breath, stilling a tremor in my belly.

Then I knocked on the door that had Dr. Ampem's name on a metal plate.

"Come in," he said.

I opened the door to the bright cool light of a fluorescent tube. Inside the room were six students, all male, staring at me. I recognized two of them from our faculty and Bangla Mensah from the SRC meetings.

For some moments, I stood frozen in the doorway.

Dr. Ampem was in his element, his face beaming.

"Come in, come in! Here is Charlotte, our first bold female!" he announced.

I took a small step in, pulling Sylvia behind me.

"Not one bold female, but two," said Dr. Ampem, his grin as wide as the joker at our concert parties.

"Come in and join my special gathering of remarkable students, with whom I discuss the country and its politics in great detail. My hope is that I am influencing a new generation of highly intellectual and capable minds who might lead Mother Ghana to glory someday," he said.

Dr. Ampem pointed Sylvia to an empty chair in the room. Then he gave me his seat behind the desk, choosing to stand against the wall where a white board hugged the wall.

It was a good thing I didn't have to say anything, because I was absolutely speechless.

The discussion was on socialism, and from time to time Dr. Ampem read from a speech given by Dr. Nkrumah to university lecturers in 1963. From the speech it was clear that Dr. Nkrumah was concerned about the abuse of academic freedom. On the one hand he promised to protect it, while giving veiled warnings about suspected abuse of such freedom.

But it was a paragraph at the end that piqued my interest.

"You who pass through the portals of our universities should be constantly aware of your oneness with the people and your responsibility towards them. This is our challenge and opportunity, and all of us — professors, teachers, alumni and students alike — must strive to maintain this great heritage which has been handed to us."

I realized that something had stirred up within me. Maybe it was hope. Maybe it was a sense of responsibility. My father once told me about his optimism at the time of Ghana's independence — the sense that as a nation they could accomplish anything and earn their place among the developed countries of the world. Everyone had felt it then.

A moment of silence passed. Then my course mates responded with a burst of applause.

At eight-thirty the meeting came to a close. Dr. Ampem asked us to wait while he locked up, and then we all walked back to the student residences in groups of two and three, still engaged in discussions.

The night was still clear, the moon was bold and a few streetlights were shining as we walked down the road.

Dr. Ampem wanted to know what I thought of the meeting.

"Frankly, sir, there was no way to expect a discussion on politics," I said.

"I know. Forgive me. I feared that you would shy away from such a group if I asked directly. And I like to test people. I can tell already that you're courageous and smart. You've seen what we do now. And if you liked this session, then please come again. You, too, Sylvia. Women have so much to offer."

Dr. Ampem hadn't brought a car, which meant he would have to walk farther than all of us, if he lived on Ridge, Okodee or Buroburo Road, where most of the lecturers lived. But he was in good spirits. Even when we parted from the others at the intersection, I could hear his laughter in the still night air.

"Wonders will never cease," said Sylvia.

‹•›

Before we knew it, term-end exams were hovering on the horizon. What I liked about Mary was her commitment to her studies, even though she was very serious about Mr. Opoku. I tried to copy her work habit, but waking up at midnight and studying till three in the morning was not at all easy to do.

Meanwhile the guys continued to troop to the eighth floor in spite of pending exams. There were times we abandoned our room to them. It seemed mean, but Mary said it was wiser to focus on our priorities. Juaben and Sylvia learned to do the same.

Then, just when I thought party time was over, there was a buzz on campus about Joe Menzie's Christmas jazz jam. Everyone said it was the party of the season, exclusively by invitation for only the coolest people.

Tall and handsome Joe Menzie was the undisputed best DJ on campus.

I was very excited to get an invitation. Young professionals were driving down from Accra, and there were four DJs for the night.

Sylvia, Juaben and I arrived around midnight. The party was already in full gear with couples scattered around the dance floor. Lampshades were wrapped in crepe paper to mute and tint the light, casting shadows in the corners of the room.

"People have gone to a lot of care to create a romantic atmosphere," said Sylvia. She turned and winked at me.

Joe Menzie was spinning. We found a table and watched people dancing. I was interested in learning new dance moves. I sipped ginger ale through a straw and laughed when Juaben pointed out a guy who had no rhythm at all.

Then I noticed Banahene leaning against the DJ's booth.

Banahene looked up and our eyes met. He came over and gave me a high-five. Then he and I danced together nice and slow to "Give Me the Night" by George Benson.

Banahene had been invited along as a guest DJ, so I went with him to the makeshift cubicle. The set-up consisted of two CD players perched on top of an amplifier and equalizer. A tiny fan was furiously blowing air to dissipate the heat from the machinery. Banahene explained that overheating could blow the amplifier.

Banahene held a headset over his left ear while he cued the follow-up song. Everyone enjoyed his selections from Chuck Mangione and Al Jarreau.

When he was satisfied that things were going well, he pulled me to my feet for a dance. I laid my head on his chest. With every breath, a hint of Brut.

And when nobody was looking, he kissed me full on the mouth.

I swallowed my surprise and let him kiss me. The kiss brought me close to tears, a strange emotion that took a while to settle.

Banahene didn't say anything before he kissed me, and he didn't say anything after. Right then, I knew that he had made a mistake, and that I wouldn't tell anyone — especially not Mary. We were just friends.

⟨•⟩

I was still recovering from the night-long party when Asare returned from his business trip to the UK. He'd been away for about a week. He was looking so sharp in a black golf shirt and gray trousers. I asked him if I could get him a drink. We had a bottle of Nkulenu orange juice in Mary's fridge — the kind one diluted in a glass of water.

"I just want a hug," he replied.

He looked a little different. It was his haircut — a high fade at the sides and back, and lined up very nicely at the front.

But there was something else, too — softness in the eyes. I looked at him a moment longer, then I gave him a hug. He brushed his lips against my cheek.

I laughed as I pulled away.

"You didn't ask for a kiss," I said.

"How you make me laugh, Charlotte. No wonder I missed you so."

"Me, too," I said. What else was one to say?

"I have something for you in my car, and then we can have a meal," he said.

Indeed, suppertime was approaching and hunger was beginning to nag at my belly. I was so pleased that we would get something good to eat in town. I perked right up.

"Okay. I'll get ready quickly, and then you can tell me everything about your trip to the UK," I said, realizing that he was the first businessman that I could call my personal friend.

I left him with Mary while I dashed to the bathroom for a shower. It would take about half an hour to get myself all fresh and changed next door. Sylvia styled my hair, oiling each curl with Ultra Sheen hair pomade until it shone. It was what I liked about relaxed hair — one could wear it straight, wavy or curled. And afro-curls were the newest craze.

I borrowed Sylvia's lilac shirt and Juaben's brown pedal pushers. I wore my brown peep-toe sandals, and Sylvia helped me with my makeup.

Sylvia said that I was deliciously pretty for the evening.

"Wow, baby," said Asare.

And I walked proudly by his side, all the way down the stairs to his car.

I settled into the coziness of The Witch. The lights on the ebony dashboard flashed as cool music wrapped around me. The AC came on, but it would be a little while before cool air chased out the humidity. I sat back and rested while Asare put the car in gear. Then we were off to the purring of the big cat BMW.

Just before we turned the corner, I saw Banahene walking towards Africa Hall. I don't know why I felt sorry for him.

We drove through Kumasi, leaving the main road for the narrow roads that looked like they had been carved out after the houses had been built. We passed by large two- and three-story houses encircled by closely hugging walls and old rusted gates. Such family houses had apartments for siblings, cousins, uncles and aunties often related to one matriarch.

Asare pointed out the boroughs of Kumasi as we left one for another. I would not be able to find my way back to campus by myself, I thought.

After a while, he said, "This is Oburonikrom."

Then he slowed down at the end of one street and turned towards a locked black gate. He honked his horn twice. I heard the sound of running feet and the jingling of a chain and then a man opened the gate, allowing Asare to drive in.

"This is my house," he said.

Unlike the huge houses we had passed on the way that took up entire plots, Asare had a large garden in front of his house.

"Come on. I just want to show you where I live. I also want to change."

"You look fine to me," I said.

He chuckled. We got out of the car and walked up the driveway.

It was a large yellow house, big and boxlike, and the windows were covered with silver burglar proofing. The garden on either side of the drive was well cultivated with flowering plants and leafy shrubs.

"I love gardens," I said.

"Let's walk around then, before we go inside. No rush, eh?"

It was on the tip of my tongue to remind him that my exams were near, but I hadn't seen him in a while. He took my hand and we went around the garden. I had always loved the hibiscus bush for its amazing red flowers and the tongue-like stamens hanging out, teasing for a kiss. I picked a flower and pushed it in my hair just above my left ear.

In the middle of the garden was my favorite childhood tree, a frangipani, shedding soft white and yellow flowers all around it. I stopped to sniff the air.

"I loved climbing that tree as a child," I said. "I could twist and turn like a gymnast on its branches."

"Tomboy, eh?" said Asare.

"Once I fell and bumped my head. I had a swelling the size of an egg just above my right eye. After that I stopped swinging on tree branches."

"Good thing!"

"Look at this one, Asare. We used to pull the tiny red flowers out like this, and suck the nectar out from the bottom."

"That's the ixora. But this yellow allamanda is poisonous, so please don't suck nectar or eat anything from it — leaf or petal."

"I'm not a child," I retorted. Although once upon a time, I might have sucked the white sap from allamanda leaves to make chewing gum. Nobody had ever said it was poisonous. Thank God I lived to know that!

"Now at last, one garden by which Kumasi can claim to be the Garden City and not the dusty city. And an owner who really knows his plants," I said.

"Hwɛ yie," warned Asare, but he reached for my hand and squeezed it.

We both laughed, and I relaxed. It was easy to like Asare, and I loved his garden. There were flower beds sculpted here and there into the grassy lawn, and a guava tree grew close to a pawpaw tree. At the back of the garden, Asare had arranged some lawn chairs and a table, and a bougainvillea bush draped itself carelessly over the wall.

"Paradise," I said. In my home we did not grow flowers — only vegetables for food.

Asare opened a side door and led me to a formal room. The furniture was gilded, and the chairs were thickly upholstered in purple, as one would expect to find in a palace. The carpet was burgundy, thick and soft.

"Sit down, please," said Asare. "Thomas, bring the lady some drinks."

I settled down into the sofa, and Thomas came bearing Star beer, Muscatella, Fanta and Coca-Cola on a tray. He also had an ice bucket, and some plantain chips and groundnut mix.

"Thank you, Thomas. I think I'll have a shandy," I said.

Deft hands found the bottle opener and snapped off bottle tops with precision. Then, tilting my glass, he filled it almost halfway with Fanta and topped it with beer.

He settled my glass beside the plate of mixed snacks on my side table. Then he left. Asare, too, excused himself and disappeared through a doorway.

Left to myself, I took little sips of my refreshment, a little worried that I might spoil my appetite for real food. I was enjoying the chase so far, but I knew that sooner or later Asare would push for me to make a commitment to him.

He came down minutes later. Surprisingly, he had changed into a white cloth. He looked very regal, down to his sturdy black Ahenemma sandals.

"Aren't we going out to dinner?" I asked.

"Why, Charlotte? Is it wrong to dine in Adinkra cloth?"

"Traditional cloth reminds me of Sunday church services and funerals," I replied. "Still, you look good. Cloth befits you really well, Prince Asare."

"The evening feels a little different to me, Charlotte," he said when he sat down. "Thomas has informed me that my mother sent apɔnkye-kakra and fufu while I've been with you at Tech. I would like to share her cooking with you, so I have asked Thomas to lay the table. If you don't mind, let us spend the evening here. We can listen to music, watch a movie or talk. I really want to chat with you."

His smile seemed genuine, even a little vulnerable as he waited for my answer.

Perhaps my face expressed doubts for he said again, "Don't worry. I am not going to be naughty."

I felt my resistance die in my throat as I took in the new Asare — chock-filled with traditional dignity. I was so reminded of my father. It was in the thick handwoven cloth, the half-bared chest, the gold neck-chain and the shiny black Ahenemma sandals. It was those snow-white shorts peeking out where the cloth parted at his every step. I was mesmerized.

Pat Thomas, Ben Brako and George Darko followed one another on a mixed popular highlife tape while we nursed our drinks. Asare told me about his trip. He had traveled to the UK and Germany on petroleum business. Although he was understated about it, I could tell it was big business.

"Is business booming for you?" I asked, trying to sound mature.

"It's a difficult business. One has to deal with corrupt government officials, shady middlemen, fierce competition and harsh OPEC conditions. It's a battle on every front.

"But you're helping Ghana through our petrol difficulties. There is no progress without power. Everything grinds to a halt when petrol is scarce," I said.

"It's not only about petrol. Kerosene is the fuel for many small mills as well as light for areas which have no electricity."

"Are there kerosene shortages?"

"Yes. Ghana's government slacks on payments, and that's the reason gas becomes scarce. Such shortages lead to speculation and inflated prices. Yet there's only so much you can borrow before creditors demand payment. I wish it was easier," he said.

"But I'm sure you're good at it," I said.

He smiled. "I have more trips coming up over Christmas. Would you like to go to the UK with me?"

"Me? You've got to be kidding."

"Just for a week or so," he said.

"I don't have a passport, and my dad would never let me go," I said.

"Never say never, Charlotte. And I can help you get a passport, no problem."

I put my glass down slowly. Getting a passport in Ghana was a big deal, and suddenly here was somebody just offering it. And not only a passport, but a trip overseas.

I had never traveled overseas. Air travel was simply too expensive for Ghana's narrow middle class, which

concentrated all its efforts on affording private preparatory schools for their children.

Just like that, all the things that seemed impossible
were tantalizingly within reach.

Soon we were settled at the table, which was set with
delicate gilt-edged china. Asare's mother's soup was piping hot and fragrant, and the fufu was pounded so soft as
to almost melt in my mouth.

Thomas waited on us until Asare permitted him to
leave. Then it was just the two of us, eating intimately like
a man and his wife. Asare asked me to dish him some more
soup, and I did so, just like I'd seen my mother do count-
less times for my father.

"This reminds me of home when Mama serves Dad his
dinner," I said.

Asare laughed, flashing fine teeth.

"I can see you as my wife, Charlotte. It wouldn't be so
bad, eh, beautiful?"

His comment sent a rush of warmth from my head to
my belly. And I laughed to hide the impact of his words
on me.

"Seriously, Charlotte, be my lady. It would be to me a
high honor."

To my surprise, I wanted to say yes. But I couldn't. And
I didn't know how to manage the silence that started right
after his unexpected semi-proposal.

"It's too fast, Asare. I don't really know you at all," I
stammered.

"What's to know, beautiful? Here I am. You may ask me
whatever you like, and whatever else you need to know,
you will find out in time."

It sounded fair, but I held back.

"Is there someone else?" he asked.

"No," I said. "But I'm not sure I'm ready."

"Okay, we'll take it slow. But don't keep me waiting too long."

I felt myself relax over supper. And then we watched a movie on VHS. Asare sat close to me on the sofa, and every now and then I felt the intensity of his gaze on me.

At ten o'clock, I asked to return to my residence. Asare stood up and drew me into his arms. I felt his warm breath on my neck. We stood for a long moment as he looked deeply into my eyes. He brought me close and brushed his lips on my cheeks. He kissed me on the lips.

Sighing, he said, "Let's go, before I lose control."

I let loose a small tinny laugh and picked up my bag and followed him to the door. We spoke little until we arrived at Africa Hall.

"Thank you very much for a lovely evening," I said, and I was surprised by the trembling in my voice.

"Didn't I say I had a gift for you?" He grabbed a shopping bag off the back seat. It was olive green and it had Harrods written across it in gold. "This is for you," he said.

"Thank you," I whispered, overcome with emotion. I leaned over and brushed his cheek with my lips. I would open it in the privacy of my room.

"See you soon, baby," he said.

I stepped out of the car and shut the door softly. I took steady steps towards the hall. I wasn't going to look back until I got to the door of Africa Hall. But I didn't have a chance to wave because The Witch sprang to life. And with a powerful roar, Asare sped away, tires hard against the gravel.

6

The following week, only a few people showed up for Dr. Ampem's Tuesday night discussion. Bangla Mensah was irritable — something about the corruption of the current government. He was exactly as I remembered him when he had argued for the student allowance at the SRC meeting — a bulldog in a fight.

"Fat party cats are stealing what remains of the wealth of this country. The shops are completely empty and everything in the market is exorbitant. To buy a common tin of evaporated milk, one needs to know the manager," he complained.

My dad had made similar comments over the years. Things had gone worse throughout the seventies with a severe lack of food and even famine. As a young teenager, I had been sent to queue for hours for bread, milk, flour and tins of sardines and corned beef. Fuel had been scarce, and Dad could spend an entire day queueing for a gallon of gas. There had been coup d'états, and the last one in 1979

73

which had brought Jerry Rawlings and the Armed Forces
Revolutionary Council to power was particularly violent.

Mensah continued his rant. "This government claims
to be socialist yet it has lost all the former gains of the
AFRC. They do not engage with the people."

This was my third meeting. I hadn't said much thus far.
I didn't even think of myself as politically engaged, but I
had a particular dislike for the AFRC.

So I spoke up. I told them about Mr. Denu, my father's
schoolmate who had been abused by AFRC cadres at his
workplace.

"They beat him and threw him into a cell at Gondar
Barracks because he dared to drive to an appointment
when they had called for a clean-up campaign. He suffered
a head injury from which he has never completely recovered. And for what?" I said.

There was a moment of silence. I guess we were getting to know where each of us stood on Ghana's political
spectrum.

Suddenly I saw it. The first divide in our politics was
between the families who thought Dr. Nkrumah was a
messiah and those who considered him a tyrant. Then
there were those who prospered under military rule —
mainly soldiers. Sometimes those belonging to the first
two groups hated each other so much, they rejoiced at a
military takeover.

"We can't throw the baby out with the bathwater,
Charlotte. Those grassroots committees did more good
than harm. Every revolution has some amount of collateral damage," said Mensah.

I didn't like his dismissive attitude. Moreover, certain

schoolmates in my secondary school had lost their fathers to revolutionary firing squads.

"I heard stories of what those AFRC cadres did in the villages. Some used their positions to get their own back on people they'd had quarrels with — even robbing and murdering those seen to be more prosperous than them. If I ever enter politics it will be to protect our citizens from such abuse," I said.

"The elite always complain about the few sporadic errors of organized grassroots. They forget that poor people die because national resources never get to them," said Mensah.

I felt the heat in my face as he twirled his pen around and around, smug as a magistrate.

"What you call grassroots politics is just clever people stirring up the working class only to hijack their power and manipulate them. Just bullies wielding cheap influence for filthy wealth. They don't fool me," I shot back.

"Charlotte, there is a real need to actively involve the grassroots in nation building. They cannot be ignored in young democracies such as ours. Dr. Nkrumah did this by means of community animators in every village and town. And they did not oppress people while doing so," said Dr. Ampem.

"Dr. Nkrumah turned Ghana from a multi-party democracy to a one-party state. He passed laws that detained his political opponents without charge," I said, sounding just like my dad.

Dr. Ampen looked directly at me. "It was the bomb threats against Dr. Nkrumah's life that led him to enforce a one-party state. It could have been a stopgap until he had gained control over the security problem. His achievements in technology and education in the few short years he governed Ghana are so remarkable. Nobody else has achieved that anywhere else in Africa."

I marveled that an astute man like Dr. Ampem was willing to make excuses for Dr. Nkrumah in spite of his abuse of democracy. But I was learning that Nkrumah had that effect on many people.

On the way back to the hall, Sylvia said, "You are good at arguing, Charlotte."

"I didn't know all these things were inside me. I guess I am my dad's daughter after all," I replied.

7

Africa Hall was particularly busy when I returned from the library the next evening. I picked my way through a crowd of people hanging around the porter's lodge and made for the stairs. I promised myself that I would find a room on the fifth floor next year and spare my leg muscles the hundred plus steps it took to get to the top floor.

Banahene was talking to Sylvia and Juaben on the eighth floor, and he followed me to my room. I threw my bag on the table and turned on the tape player, but "Get Down On It," hardly seemed appropriate for an early-evening conversation.

"I should get you some jazz," said Banahene.

He rummaged through the small tape collection we kept in a shoebox. He found another tape and inserted it, filling our space with the sound of instrumental music.

It was so easy to be around Banahene. My mind returned to that one kiss that night at the party. Perhaps in some strange way, he had needed to get that out of the way to continue on with our friendship.

I told Banahene about my meeting with Dr. Ampem's group. I was giving a blow-by-blow account of the verbal sparring with Bangla Mensah when I heard the key turn in the lock. Mary was home.

"Roomie, are you decent? Guess who's here?" Mary called out cheerfully as she pushed the door open.

Asare came in right after her, knocking my guesses right out of my mouth.

"Whassup, baby?" Asare said.

I winced. That accent continued to be the one thing that embarrassed me about him.

Before I could respond, he saw Banahene. Asare's lips tightened, killing his smile. I expected Banahene to crack one of his jokes to ease the awkwardness, but he didn't. Instead he seemed to spread himself a little wider, as he placed his arms squarely on the wooden arms of the chair.

I looked from one to the other. Asare stood upright and taut except for the car keys he twirled round and round on his index finger. I felt the heat climbing up my neck.

Thankfully, Mary recovered quickly and made the introductions.

"Asare, meet my cousin Banahene."

Asare's eyes narrowed, but he greeted Banahene politely.

Banahene neither stood up nor offered his hand when he replied. This made things even more awkward. I gave my chair to Asare and went and sat by Mary on the lower bunk. It felt crowded in the room.

Asare declined a drink. Banahene accepted one, and

Mary and I kept up the chatter like two skilled tennis players keeping a ball in play.

Thankfully, ten minutes later, Asare said he was leaving. So I walked him down the stairs, leaving Banahene with Mary.

Asare was a little shaken.

"Charlotte, I just thought I'd surprise you, you know. So I jumped at the chance to drop Mary off for Opoku. Sorry if I disturbed you."

"You didn't disturb me. Banahene is Mary's cousin," I replied.

"Really?"

"Yes," I said emphatically.

"That boy could have fooled me. He was acting like your boyfriend," Asare insisted.

"How?"

"Just the way he sat there with some authority. Small-boy like him," scoffed Asare.

"It's just his way," I said.

"Dwɛɛ!"

I laughed. "Banahene is Ashanti, full of brash bravado, just like you."

Asare's raised eyebrow meant he didn't believe me one bit. We lingered at the lobby. Then he took my hand in his as we strolled out towards his car.

"I actually wanted to take you out for a little while, because I kind of hijacked that last date," he said. And the memory of that evening flooded me to my toes with warmth. My heart quickened.

"We can do that another time. I haven't even showered," I said softly.

"How about I come back in an hour?" he pressed, eyes fixed intently on me. Even his keys lay still in his hand.

I realized that he wanted to prove something — that he could carry off the prize of the night. There was something I liked about that.

"Okay, I'll be ready in an hour. Don't come up to get me. I'll be waiting downstairs," I said at last.

A smile lit up his face. "Thanks for saving me from those stairs. And, baby, wear the dress I bought you," he whispered.

"Not tonight," I replied.

"Why do you have so much fire in you?"

"Why do you want to douse it?"

"Not at all, baby. I just want to share it. I like you just the way you are."

⟨•⟩

No sooner did I get back to my room than Banahene stood up on his feet.

"I'm off now, ladies," he announced brightly.

"I'm not walking down those stairs again," I said.

"Come off it, Charlotte. You never see me off beyond the verandah," he said.

Quietly, he let himself out of our room and the door clicked shut behind him. We listened as his footsteps faded away.

"I've never seen Banahene like that. Is there something going on between you two?" Mary asked.

But I couldn't bring myself to tell her that we had kissed. It felt like a betrayal to share it. Then I had to hurry along because Asare was coming back to fetch me in an hour.

"Girl, you should have let him climb back again to prove his love. You've got to let guys sweat in the chase, because after that it's plain sailing for them all the way," said Mary.

But I knew she was pleased that Asare was coming back. Mary preferred established men.

Thankfully, the shower was working and I was in and out in ten minutes. I was running out of clever combinations to wear.

I thought about Asare's gift. In the Harrods bag was a pretty dress and a bottle of perfume — Chanel No. 5. The dress was a crinkly, red and blue floral polyester — sleeveless and simple but sophisticated. I had tried it on once but it felt awkward to wear a dress that a man other than my dad had bought for me. I did not want to give him the impression that I was all his, just yet.

So I wore my beloved Huggers jeans again, with a simple black shirt. I did my makeup carefully, applying lipgloss over a dark purple lipstick. A dab of Chanel was my only concession.

"What do you think?" I asked Mary.

"Beautiful," she replied, and set my heart at ease.

The challenge was to walk down all those stairs in high heels. I was so concentrated on placing my feet right that I didn't notice the person coming down behind me.

"Charlotte," he said.

I froze. It was Banahene, again.

"Going out?" he asked.

"Yes," I said, holding tightly onto the banister.

"I went to collect my textbook from Rosemary," he said.

"Have you got something going on with Rosemary?" I asked.

"What?" he said.

We continued in silence down three flights of stairs, my heels clicking uneasily against the concrete.

"Have fun," he said when we got to the lobby.

"Thanks," I replied. Then I sat on the stone bench beside the latticed wall of the lobby and watched as Banahene left the hall.

Why did I feel so guilty?

A few minutes later, I was washed in the glare of bright headlights. Then I heard the unmistakable sound of a BMW coming to a halt.

There was Asare, right on time.

⟨•⟩

We went to City Hotel, and I ordered the club sandwich with fries. It was the easiest thing to do in my state of mind.

"Make that two and a Star beer," said Asare.

"Muscatella for me," I said.

Asare was different — a little subdued, and I was feeling low from the evening's confrontations.

I looked around me. Same old weathered curtains and wobbly tables in the dining room, and a scratchy highlife record playing. Someone had shut off the air conditioner, and a standing fan stood in the corner blasting warm air.

I had to try to make some conversation to save the date.

"I'm in this discussion group, and we're kind of political," I said.

"Tell me about it."

And so I told Asare about Dr. Ampem, Mensah and the others.

"I know Ampem. Socialist," snorted Asare. "He had some connections to the AFRC government, and I'm sure he's still converting students to his beliefs. Be careful."

"You don't like socialists?"

"I'm a businessman. We do all this work raising capital against collateral. We design supply chain processes and implement them. We employ people and pay taxes. We want our profits."

I wanted to ask him more about his political views — what he thought about the poor and underserviced. But I didn't want to stress the evening further.

"Tell me more about your business. Do you own gas stations in Ghana?"

"We don't own gas stations. Primo Oil and Gas buys and sells petroleum products, natural gas and natural gas liquids. It's a midstream industry so we deal with storage and transportation of petroleum products from product source to certain countries. The upstream industry finds and produces crude oil and natural gas, and the downstream industries are involved with distribution and retail."

"You're a middleman," I said. In Ghana middlemen were associated with kalabule, the illegal hiking of prices.

"You look disappointed. People like me are responsible for sourcing and shipping gas to Ghana even before Shell, BP and GOIL make it available at the pumps. What we do is crucial. We deal with the government, mainly."

"Do you make a lot of money?" I asked.

Asare laughed. "It depends on what you think a lot of money looks like. But I want to eat with you and not talk business," he said.

The waiter had appeared with our food and so we ate. Afterwards we returned to the car. Asare put the key in the switch and turned to me.

"You should have worn the dress I bought you."

"Another time," I said.

"Charlotte. Don't you like me?"

"I do."

"But I love you."

He reached for me and pulled me close to him. He began to kiss me. It was a bit uncomfortable in a car with such low seats, but I kissed him back.

"Be my girlfriend, darling. I promise you, it will be good."

"Just give me till the end of the term to decide, please. Everything is very new right now," I said.

"Till the end of the term, Charlotte. Choose me and you'll never regret it," he said, tracing a line across my lip with his index finger.

⟨•⟩

December brought mixed feelings. I was excited at the thought of the Christmas holidays, but one had to get through the end of term to get to the holidays. With pocket money gone and food stores depleted, our student allowance just wouldn't stretch to cover the fortnight for which it was allocated. If Bangla Mensah had brought his motion to the SRC in December, it would have passed without a doubt.

Exams were very close. I had less than two weeks to cram all the term's work before exams. I had gone to all the parties and received the boys who came night after night to Dɔ-me-a-bra — where people go for love — the nickname for Africa Hall.

Now my afternoons were all about the library, where I competed with others to find the right books to study. But my joy at finding a book would soon turn into despair, when I discovered chunks of chapters ripped out by selfish students.

I stayed out late at the library and missed Asare's goodbye visit before he left again for Europe. He had left a package for me at the porter's lodge. Inside the large brown envelope were passport forms, an airline ticket from Kumasi to Accra, some money, as well as a note.

My darling Charlotte, fill the passport forms today and let Willie have them. I have a trip planned for us in the New Year. Since I won't be there to take you home when school ends, take the flight from Kumasi airport. The hassle with STC buses is dreadful at this time of the year. I should be back on the 3rd of January. Too bad I'm going to miss celebrating the holidays with you. I can't wait to hold you in my arms.

It ended: *I love you, Charlotte. Remember that. Asare.*

I was overwhelmed. What I felt for him could only be love, and the money was the cure-all for my end-of-term blues.

I was ready to become Asare's girlfriend. He so easily made me feel good. I wondered if people might think I was with him because he was rich. But when it was all said and done, Asare was a really nice guy. And we got on fabulously.

⟨•⟩

Exam week. Mr. Opoku gave Mary a break from his visits and Banahene stayed away, engrossed in his own work. The porters smiled more, happy that we were connecting with our purpose and not flaunting the high life in their faces.

"Good luck," Mr. Afriyie would say to me each time I left the hall with the stress of exams etched in my eyes. In the meantime, general food shortages strengthened our friendships and interdependence on the eighth floor. In Room 803, between Mr. Opoku and Asare, we were very well supplied. I followed Mary's example of generosity and shared what we had with everyone.

The days passed and I finished paper after paper. Sometimes I was elated, other times deflated. I was always short of sleep. My political science papers were okay. One English paper was very difficult.

I could imagine my dad saying, "What? A weak mark in English. Didn't you go to Achimota School?"

I discussed the English paper with Sylvia, and felt worse than before.

Mary said, "Never discuss a paper that's behind you."

Then slowly, as the term drew to an end, I felt the pressure lift off. Christmas was near.

8

School closed for the Christmas holidays, and Sylvia and Juaben caught the STC bus in town for Accra. They had to leave campus before 4 a.m. to get a good spot in the queue.

Mary's trip home was the easiest. She packed her bags and drove to Nhyiaeso with Mr. Opoku. Mr. Opoku returned for me that afternoon and dropped me off at the airport.

I was excited about flying for the first time. I even considered wearing the dress Asare gave me, but in the end I wore my trusted jeans because I didn't want my mother asking questions.

I felt the shaking as the engines came alive. Then the plane rushed down the runway and lifted us off the ground. My eyes followed the clutter of buildings which became smaller and more distant until they gave way to the green of the forest and the little villages that huddled in them. We climbed until we overtook the clouds.

"Expect turbulence," the pilot warned five minutes into the flight. And I held on to my belly when it somersaulted between my chest and my knees.

Thirty minutes later, we were touching down in Accra to the sound of rushing wind.

"Thank you, Asare," I whispered.

‹•›

We sat around the old dining table which Sarah had laid for dinner. Mama's checkered square cloth had been spread diagonally on the table leaving some of the wood exposed. It was her way of making do with a small tablecloth.

To welcome me home, Mama had cooked Jollof rice, and she heaped my bowl to the brim.

"Tell me about university," said Dad between mouthfuls of spicy orange rice.

I told him about my lectures and lecturers. I told him about my exams and a little bit about my girlfriends. But I didn't say anything about the guys. And I was not going to tell my parents about flying home on Asare's ticket. That would have been disastrous.

"Your hair, Charlotte. You look pretty," said Mama, brushing my hair with her hand.

Dad said nothing, and Sarah winked at me.

All I wanted was for my parents to acknowledge that I was old enough to have some privileges — the kind that gave me access to some night life in Accra.

Later on, Sarah and I lay side by side on the bed we'd shared for years. We talked deep into the night. She wanted to hear about varsity — my friends, the parties and the ponding. I swore her to secrecy and told her about flying home in an airplane.

That made her eyes pop.

‹•›

Christmas Day came five days later. In Accra, it was mainly about festive feasting. Mama fetched our tired artificial tree and dressed it up with tinsel. I got a pair of navy blue pumps and a ready-made dress for presents, and nobody pretended it was from Father Christmas. I wore the dress to Mass. We lit candles and sang the old carols.

Afterwards we came home, received guests and ate. We visited uncles, aunties and good friends, and we ate the same things in each house — Huntley and Palmers Gem Biscuits, bottles of Fanta and Coca-Cola, Mama's chicken light soup with fufu, Jollof rice with beef, and custard and cake.

The rest of the week was a blur of visits, visitors, good will and peace on earth.

I had a plan for the 31st of December. Sylvia, Juaben and I had invitations to two parties — one at the Airport Residential Area, and the other at Ringway Estates, Osu.

The only hurdle that stood between me and a good time was my dad.

‹•›

Dad was writing at his desk. I couldn't think of any other way to do it so I went up to him, one adult to another, and just told him my plan.

He looked at me over his reading glasses, and the lines on his forehead were deeper than ever.

"New Year's Eve should be given to contemplation and prayers for the coming year. It isn't a good night to be out. There will be many drunk drivers on the road, tempting fate," he said.

He returned to the notepad he'd been writing on, and I heard him mumble something under his breath.

"Dad, I'm a big girl. I am not going driving with drunken people."

"Charlotte, I am saying no! Don't you have any respect for me?"

I realized he was working himself up to an explosive blow-out that would take days to settle.

Finally, I said, "What's the point, Dad? You don't live with me on my campus in Kumasi. Even if we stick to your rules when I'm home, what can you do about me when I'm in Kumasi?"

My boldness stunned him into momentary silence. Then he found his voice again.

"I should hope you appreciate the good morals taught you in this house, Charlotte Adom."

"Yes, Dad, that's about it. You can only hope," I replied softly.

Something made Dad swallow his next words. I watched as his tense shoulders went slack and frown lines faded from his face.

Right then, I knew I had won my right to go out on New Year's Eve.

‹•›

What I did not expect was sickness. After lunch nausea crept over me like a shadow and rested in my chest. I felt a whisper of pain in my belly. The pain increased in waves until sweat bathed me from head to toe.

I couldn't tell Dad or Mama. That would have been the end of my plans.

I was crouched on the bed when Sarah found me.

"Are you sick?" she asked.

"Don't tell anyone," I whispered.

"Is it your period?"

"Tummy ache — maybe indigestion."

"If you can throw up, you'll be fine," said Sarah.

I was willing to try anything, so Sarah got two eggs from the fridge and whipped them up with a full tin of Ideal milk.

"This will make you vomit," she said, thrusting a cup into my hand.

I pinched my nostrils and swallowed. I gagged as it forced its way down my throat.

"Let's go to the bathroom. Then you can stick a finger down your throat," said Sarah authoritatively.

"But they'll hear me," I whined.

"Don't worry. I'll shut the door and put the radio on loud."

We took the radio to the bathroom and turned it on. I bent over the toilet and stuck my forefinger down far enough. I retched but nothing came up.

I was about to try again, when the music on GBC 2 stopped abruptly.

"This is Flight Lieutenant Jerry John Rawlings. Fellow citizens of Ghana, as you would have noticed we are not playing the national anthem. In other words this is not a coup. I ask for nothing less than a revolution, something that would transform the social and economic order of this country. There is no justice in this society and so long as there is no justice, I would dare say let there be no peace."

I retched, then, and vomited.

Just like that, the PNP government of Dr. Limann was overthrown. There would be no parties that night in the beloved country.

⟨•⟩

At eighteen years old, I had already experienced four coup d'états in my lifetime. I was too young to remember anything about February 24, 1966, when Dr. Nkrumah's government was ousted, but I could still remember January 13, 1972, when Colonel Acheampong booted Dr. Busia's Progress Party from power. My memory was clear only because my parents had never ceased to bemoan the sudden turn of events, for they'd had such hope in Dr. Busia. At that time my mother's cousin — the most influential person in her family — lost his job as a director of the Cocoa Marketing Company of Ghana. He never recovered, and an early stroke sent him heaven bound. At ten and a half years old, I understood that a coup d'état was a sudden swift change that cast people at the top of the social ladder headlong to the bottom, establishing a new order.

But it was June 4, 1979, that I remembered most clearly — the first time Rawlings came to power. Our former national leaders, all military men, were tried in quickly convened military courts and executed by firing squad. General Acheampong and General Utuka were the first to be executed, and then the others followed. I was schoolmates with the children of a number of those who were killed in those days of terror. Consequently, I developed a distaste for military takeovers.

So now I wondered what would happen in these new days of revolution. My parents' jobs as teachers were unlikely to get them any attention. It was mainly the important people in high positions and wealthy businessmen who attracted persecution.

But my dad was worried.

"Anyone can become a target with these bloodthirsty soldiers. Two years ago anything could bring on a beating or a shooting. You just needed to cross one of them on a bad day. Say somebody did not like the price of a shirt, a piece of fabric, or a bowl of koko. That could turn very ugly in moments."

Mama said, "All it took was for a complaint to be made to a soldier — and there were often several walking about town. He would arrive, cock his gun at the offender and perhaps shoot it. The best outcome would be a beating with the butt of the gun. This was happening in the small towns and villages as well as the cities. But the press hardly reported anything from the villages."

So there was no joy or peace, even when we wished each other a Happy New Year.

Days passed. Dad was torn between keeping me at home and sending me back to school. He was never out of earshot of his radio, whether he was out in the yard tending chickens or sitting at the table eating lunch. I could hear the murmurings of the radio, intermittently eclipsed by high-pitched static. And I could hear him muttering beneath his breath, "Dɛn asɛm ni — what trouble! How did we sleep, unconcerned, until the return of this wretched man?"

The wretched man was Jerry Rawlings. But this time around, his government was called the Provisional National Defence Council.

Each day, people made their way cautiously to work and back. They formed polite queues at the taxi stations. There was no cheating and no hustling. Easily given apologies were the order of the day if one was accused of any transgression. It was as if eyes were watching. This is what my mother said as she returned daily from the primary school where she taught.

A week passed. It appeared that the times were not as dangerous as two years previously, when Rawlings' AFRC had come into power. Perhaps the army was showing more restraint this time.

I kept my ears peeled for news of our university's re-opening. I talked to some friends who lived nearby and who attended the University of Ghana at Legon. There were no announcements about closing colleges.

So on the 10th of January, as soon as the 6 p.m. to 6 a.m. curfew lifted, Dad drove me to the STC station to catch a bus to Kumasi.

Dad was a cautious driver on an ordinary day. Now I feared that we might be stopped for crawling like a caterpillar on the road.

There wasn't much traffic that early in the morning. Here and there, soldiers in their olive green uniforms and police in their black uniforms stood in small groups, just watching.

There were no street hawkers at the lights; not even beggars hustling. We had passed by only two mad men in tattered clothing with dirty matted hair. Perhaps mad men were the only ones who feared nothing in the new revolution.

Dad let out a sigh of relief as we turned into the station. It was sad to see him so afraid.

He parked his Peugeot 404 at the dusty carpark which was ravaged by potholes. He helped me to the ticket booths with my luggage. He carried my suitcase while I carried my sports bag. It was the first time I was going away to school without a box of tinned foods — milk, sardines or corned beef — nonperishable food that students depended on for those long months away from home.

"A sign of the times," my mother had said.

But Dad gave me some money, and it was reassuring to bump into some Tech students at the station.

Dad was reluctant to leave me there.

"I'll be okay, Dad. Mama will be wondering where you are."

He knew I was right. I watched him as he headed for the carpark. I saw him hovering around his car and waved him away.

"Just go, Dad. The ticket booth is open and we'll leave soon," I said.

As if on cue, two green-and-white buses entered the loading bay, and I rushed with the others to join the queue at the booth.

A commotion started near the front of the line. A man was called out by some soldiers for trying to jump the queue. It was hard to watch as he received ear-stopping slaps. Thankfully they let him go, and he rejoined the queue at the tail end. Nobody said anything. These were days of revolution.

I was so glad Dad had left already. He might have changed his mind and returned me home after that violent incident.

I saw Sylvia up ahead in the queue. If we could get tickets for the same bus perhaps we'd be able to sit together.

Finally at 8 a.m. we boarded the bus. We sat comfortably, one person to a seat — not crammed in like sardines as we used to travel before the revolution.

Just on the outskirts of Accra a barrier had been mounted by armed soldiers. One of the soldiers flagged our coach down and demanded to search the hold.

For a while it seemed as if we would all have to dismount and open our bags for a search. But our driver went to see the commander in the booth. He paid a bribe and soon we were on our way.

Our driver told us they were looking for suspicious citizens who were fleeing the country. One did not have to be corrupt to flee. The kangaroo courts of 1979 were still fresh in our memories for sending members of the old government to their deaths.

I remembered how my dad had grieved over the mistreatment of his hometown's best-known entrepreneur, Mr. Siaw of Tata Brewery, who lost all his business assets to state confiscation. Then there was Mr. B.A. Mensah who had suffered several arrests leading to the seizure of his tobacco company.

Our driver had to stop at every barrier on the road. Passengers grumbled among themselves as the journey dragged on. Sylvia was on the bus, but sitting up ahead. So in keeping with my dad's advice, I didn't engage in any conversations with strangers. I just closed my eyes and allowed my mind to wander. Was Asare back yet? Mary would know. I couldn't wait to see my friends in Africa Hall.

At the truck stop at Nkawkaw, Sylvia and I shared hot fried yam and pepper sauce, and a bottle of Fanta. She told me that the 31st night party-makers had fled the country.

"Imagine if we had been out jamming when the coup occurred," she said. "The army may have rounded us all up."

We found a table in the gloomy cafeteria. Next to us, a group of men were talking over a shared bowl of banku and okro stew.

"J.J. must be a lucky fellow. I swear — the man must have some strong juju!"

"Strong-o! How many people go from facing death to two-time head of state," said the other man, after gulping down some beer.

An older man passing between our tables paused long enough to add a thought. "Certainly, he is luckier than all the previous heads of state. Three of them lie dead by the firing squads of his AFRC."

9

Kumasi was quieter than Accra. I was happy to see Mary, and couldn't wait to trade stories. She told me Asare was still overseas.

Calls by bush telephone were incessant as Africa Hall filled over the weekend. We were checking on one another as though one among us might be missing. Juaben's bus had been delayed for a full hour at the Accra barrier, and soldiers had arrested a man on their wanted list.

Out there, life was crazy. But the university was our world, and we began to settle down once our lectures started.

On Mr. Opoku's first visit to see Mary, he brought me a package in a brown envelope.

It was my brand new passport. It had been given to him by Asare's contact just before Christmas. I opened the passport and rifled through the pages. I wished the picture were more complimentary, but it was still me and my details were correct.

Just like that, I owned a passport, and it was now possible for Asare to take me overseas. My heart skipped a beat. Dad would never allow that — not unless I sneaked out of the country while I was supposed to be in school.

I thought about it, and suddenly I knew I could do it.

"Thank you, Mr. Opoku," I said.

"Asare is a man of good intentions," he said.

"Yes, but when is he coming back?"

"Aha, you miss him. Tell the truth now," said Mr. Opoku, beaming. "He's going to wait in the UK for things to settle down here. Give him a month. His business is the kind that always comes under much scrutiny. He's lucky the coup happened while he was away. There are people who would wish him harm."

"What about you? Are you safe?" I asked Mr. Opoku.

"As safe as the next person," he replied.

I was curious about Asare's enemies, but Mr. Opoku wouldn't say much. I could not get any information beyond what I already knew. Asare basically shipped petroleum to Ghana. He had talked about corrupt government officials. He had hinted that petroleum could be dangerous business.

"Penny for your thoughts," said Mary, watching Mr. Opoku. A sudden faraway look had entered his eyes.

"It's wise to say very little right now. Kumasi is a very unhealthy town," said Mr. Opoku softly.

"What do you mean? I thought it was quieter here than Accra," I said.

"Many businesses are on lockdown until the mood of the revolution calms down. Ordinary people are reporting on their neighbors out of sheer jealousy. Soldiers have their eyes on people's properties. If you have a little more than your neighbor you're in trouble. I have parked my Mercedes-Benz and am using my mother's Golf. Hmm, Kumasi!" said Mr. Opoku.

I remembered the flight I had taken home for the Christmas holidays. It had taken only thirty-five minutes from Kumasi to Accra. My recent trip by road was seven hours long. Nobody would dare use the airports now for internal flights. It had become a curse to appear prosperous in Ghana.

"We've got to be careful, even on campus. You know the saying. Walls have ears," said Mary.

"Campus is still safer than town," I insisted.

"But nobody knows for how long. Please, just don't join any alutas," said Mr. Opoku. University students in Ghana were known for demonstrations whenever they felt they had a cause.

The aroma of stewed tomatoes, shrimp and ginger filled the room. I waited with anticipation for the Jollof rice Mary was cooking. Mary dished out for Mr. Opoku, and then for me. And the three of us shared a most delicious meal. Good food had the power to soothe my uneasiness.

Mr. Opoku left soon after. There would be no more outings for us for a while, and no more visits late into the night. Rawlings' government had imposed a 6 p.m. curfew across the length and breadth of the country. It was far safer to lie low in one's home than to be seen here and there, enjoying the good life.

‹•›

At the university we could walk about at any time, so long as we did not go off campus. This was our city, insulated from the rest of the country. So the usual traffic between halls started again.

As someone had said, "All roads lead to Africa!"

Banahene came to visit that evening, and this time there was no competition with externals — the boyfriends who were not university students. I gave him the warmest hug, and he returned my enthusiasm with a kiss on the cheek. His eyes twinkled with mischief as we caught up with each other.

"Have you observed the effects of this coup d'état? So many students have turned socialist."

"How do you know? We haven't had an SRC meeting yet," I said.

"Haven't you seen them striding about in Black Moses sandals, calling each other comrade?" he asked, referring to the rough-and-ready sandals cut out of old car tires.

I checked out Banahene's shoes. They were brown-leather lace-up shoes. He also had on a blue shirt with sleeves rolled up to his biceps.

He was no socialist if clothes were the sign.

"If these people have their own way, Black Moses may become standard wear by law — the people's sandals!"

‹•›

It was Tuesday, and we had gathered in Dr. Ampem's office for the first of our group meetings for the term. I had gone with Sylvia as usual. We found the group enlarged by three others. Jordan, my lanky course mate who had won the discussion over the Dawn Broadcast, had come for the very first time.

Behind his black-framed spectacles, Dr. Ampem's eyes danced with passion. His hair had grown thicker over the break. His beard was still small and scruffy, and he had full charge of the agenda.

"There are now possibilities for real change at the grassroots," he said. "We can finish what was started in 1979, at the awakening of the people."

I had never heard him associate so closely with Rawlings' 1979 coup.

"Sir, do you mean that you prefer a military government to a civilian government?" I asked.

"No, Charlotte. It was Marx who said revolutions are the locomotives of history. It usually takes the power of militancy to birth a revolution. Then they must access the power of intellectuals to determine the forward momentum. I believe in government for and of the people, but not when it is hijacked by special interest — particularly selfish capitalist interest. If Dr. Nkrumah had been alive, we might have brought him back at this historic time. But instead here we are."

There it was again — the royal we. I couldn't let it go.

"Sir, are you not worried that the military will mistreat the people as they did in 1979? People are scared, wondering if there are more executions waiting to happen," I said.

"Charlotte, trust me, there will be no bloodshed this time. This is a controlled exercise. It is not reactionary. There is a real agenda to put this nation forward. In fact, the times have become intensely exciting, and some of you should be stepping up as the next SRC leaders when the current council hands over. I hope that this group of ours has prepared you for leadership and provided you with some basis for ideology."

Commitment burned in his eyes like red hot embers inside a coal pot. Ampem's ownership of the current government was as strong as if he had held a gun alongside the coup makers.

A chill traveled down my spine.

Bangla Mensah began to suggest names for formalizing our group into a committee. He settled on the Socialist Students' Think Tank. Mensah had adopted Ampem's way of using the royal we. He was talking as if he had some clout with the new government.

Dr. Ampem asked if I would like to be secretary or treasurer.

"You might even stand as president. It's time for new things," he said with a loud chuckle. But Mensah did not laugh.

"I'll think about it, sir," I replied.

"The changes which are coming are monumental, and we shall need courageous leaders to harness the energy of the youth. There has never been such an opportunity for Ghana," said Bangla Mensah.

Suddenly I realized it was Mensah's intention to use our group as a base for his own stand on campus.

My own father was not on the left half of the political divide, and neither was my mother. Like them I understood the importance of welfare but I was not attracted to the authoritarian way of life of the Russians or the Chinese. They had no freedom.

Also my parents were strongly opposed to military governments, even if they were too scared to utter a word about it in the daylight. I was worried because Dr. Ampem made it sound as though we were already an arm of the PNDC revolution. I made up my mind to tell Sylvia that I was quitting.

On our way back that evening, Sylvia chose to walk with Mensah, and I kept company with Dr. Ampem and the others.

Back at Africa Hall, Sylvia had news for me.

"Mensah just asked me to go out with him," she said, unable to contain her joy.

"Mensah?" I said, stunned.

"Yes. He is my boyfriend."

It was then I realized that I was on my own.

‹•›

Dr. Ampem missed class the next Thursday, and the class disintegrated into groups of noisy conversations. Jordan had a newspaper, and we read about the dismissals and arrests of men in high office. There were no reasons given for the sacking of several career diplomats and civil servants, except to accuse them vaguely of inefficiency.

Clearly, the new government was making room for its own breed of civil servants.

The center pages of the newspaper were dedicated to J.J. Rawlings. In one picture he was bent over a spade unclogging an open drain. In another picture he was on a podium spouting his ideas of revolution. He was always surrounded by cheering crowds and the usual faces of his

PNDC comrades. The picture had a caption: *Rawlings' ideology is summed up in one word, Ghana.*

Just before the period ended, Jordan asked me, "Are you going to the SRC meeting on Saturday?"

"Why don't we invite the class?" I stood up and addressed the class. "People, there is going to be an SRC meeting on the weekend. This is one we shouldn't miss. I appeal to the ladies, especially. We need to make our voices heard."

"This is the time to speak up," said Jordan.

"We will be there," said my course mate Philomena.

For the first time I identified significant interest in student politics among my course mates. I remembered that first debate we'd had about noise as a public nuisance on campus. Only a few of us had spoken then, but the coup d'état had triggered something in the air.

‹•›

For lunch, Sylvia, Juaben and I went over to the food base across the road from the social sciences faculty. It was a hot day and we found a bench beneath the tree. I wanted to eat waakye — purple rice and beans. The others opted for fried plantain and beans. I preferred to have my food wrapped in leaves rather than a poorly washed, oily bowl.

"African germs don't kill," said Juaben, who received her food in an orange plastic bowl.

"Nonsense," I said.

I was delighted to see Banahene as he and some guys crossed the road to the food base. He left the guys and joined us after he had bought a serving of gari and beans with a drizzle of thick zomi palm oil. He sat astride the narrow bench and tucked into his food. A flock of crows crossed the afternoon sky, cawing as they went by.

"Did you girls know that Dr. Ampem belongs to a powerful socialist fraternity in Accra? He is apparently good buddies with Rawlings. It makes sense that he was starting some kind of cell here. Charlotte, you and Sylvia may be on some list of socialist revolutionaries," said Banahene dramatically.

"You hype everything through the roof, Banahene," said Sylvia.

"Dr. Ampem would have told us," I said.

"Why does he have to hide anything? He has nothing to fear," said Sylvia.

Still, I remembered the way he used the pronoun we at our last meeting.

A sudden shout at a nearby table interrupted our discussion.

"This can't be true. No way!" said one of the guys.

"What's up?" shouted Banahene.

"Daavi, turn up the radio," said someone to the waakye seller.

We all gathered around the small radio that stood on the serving table. One of the guys fiddled with the tuner. Moments later, we heard the announcement.

"The government has closed down all the universities and tertiary institutions in the country. Students are to proceed to their homes and await instructions from the National Service Secretariat."

It appeared we were being sent home to engage in exercises to rescue the country. The main agenda was to evacuate cocoa, which apparently was languishing in the interior for failure of transportation.

We were stunned.

Everywhere along the Mecca road, students were talking about it. Back in the hall, the news traveled along the corridors and across the courtyard by bush telephone.

That evening the news was posted on the notice boards in every hall and every department. We could talk until we were hoarse, but the government was forcing us all into the rainforest to transport the cocoa harvest to the various ports of Ghana.

Over the weekend we said our goodbyes. We were all hoping it wouldn't be long before we returned to school. We packed our belongings. I was so glad when Mary agreed to take most of my boxes to her home. Then, along with Sylvia, Juaben and Banahene, I caught the STC bus for Accra.

The revolution had come home to me.

10

In Accra, we received our first instructions by radio. Students from my part of the city were to meet on the grounds of a local elementary school. We milled around, confused and full of complaints. Eventually Elias Dagadu, a third-year student from the University of Ghana, Legon, and a member of their SRC took charge. Dagadu was a serious-looking fellow with buck teeth. He wrote our names against the university or college we attended, and the year of matriculation. Then he sent us off in teams to pick up litter.

At noon we were sent home. Our new instructions were to bring brooms and machetes for the rest of the week.

The next day they carried us in trucks to an illegal rubbish dump near Nima. If there was a hell on earth, this was it, and our task was to cleanse hell.

There were about fifty students in our work team. We were given shovels to move the rubbish — rotting food, decomposing rodents, even human excreta — onto a truck. The smell alone could have killed me.

We worked without gloves or boots, and at day's end we could hardly bear to be near each other. I didn't even entertain the idea of lunch, and I was thankful for the standing-room-only truck ride back home. Sitting would have pressed my clothes against my body, and pressed others against me.

When I got home, Dad fetched the garden hose and hosed me down right there in the front yard. As for my shoes and clothes, my mother threw them away that evening.

In Accra, all tertiary students had been organized into similar neighborhood groups. The rumor was that if we did not check in with our particular groups daily, we would not be able to check back into university. Our groups had been announced on the radio. But it was never quite clear to me if we were being managed by the National Union of Ghana Students or the National Service Secretariat, which administered the obligatory year of service graduates rendered to the country for covering our tertiary education.

On the plus side of things, I reconnected with some students I knew from Tech and also from my former secondary school. I also made new acquaintances. All this while we picked up litter and cleared unkempt bushes.

Meanwhile, I imagined that socialists like Dr. Ampem were hard at work designing plans in tight think tanks to transition Marxist theories into the mainstream.

Many of us were opposed to these exercises, but because we were unwilling to risk our places at the university, we went exactly where we were told.

ALUTA

Nothing irked my parents more than the radio announcements that were posted about student mobilization.

"Nkwaseasɛm — nonsense!" said my dad. "To think your studies have been halted so you can sweep around places for which people have been hired to clean. Imagine a stupid claim that we are unable to move our most important cash crop to the ports. Tweaa! So much foolishness in one country! We might as well bring back the colonizers!"

I agreed with him. With so many unemployed people, why would the government close down the universities and insist on student labor to move cocoa from the forest to the port? Didn't they realize that they were taking jobs away from seasonal workers?

We had worked for a week when they announced to us that our group was one of those being sent to Kwahu to move cocoa. These were the days of martial law, and there was nothing for it but to comply.

‹•›

No matter which direction one took out of Accra, the countryside was the same — half-cement, half-adobe houses scattered among dilapidated mud hovels. Scruffy children played in the dust, and tired men and women walked with various loads on their heads, sweating in the sun. Our bus wheezed on the climb up the narrow twisting road.

I rested my head against the window, three seats behind the driver. Nothing changed from mile to mile — not even the dusty bushes that grew between villages.

110

In our bus, the male students were singing songs, and one of them was clicking a thumb-bell to keep the rhythm. The rhythm-keeper was the leader — a smallish man in a red beret who sang profanities in a falsetto. I wished I could zone out completely, but it was impossible on this crowded ride up the Kwahu Mountains towards the town of Obo. Like an aging asthmatic the bus slowed to a crawl when the road became too steep.

"I hope the engine doesn't die on us," I muttered.

"Don't worry," said the girl who sat next to me. "There are enough stupid songs to urge it on forever."

I couldn't help but smile. I turned to her and said, "Hello. I am Charlotte from Tech."

"Sharon from Cape Coast University," she replied.

She had been trying to read Jacqueline Susann's *Valley of the Dolls*. But like me she'd had to quit. The power rested with those turning good songs into profanity.

The women who sat in front of me were shouting just to hear each other. Sharon closed her eyes and tried to sleep. I watched the trees, which we left behind at thirty miles an hour.

Finally, after three hours of incessant noise, I'd had enough. I stood up and shouted to the backbenchers, "Shut up!"

I heard Sharon draw in her breath. There was a moment of silence. Then a low growl grew to a crescendo, and I was soon swallowed up in a full-scale secondary-school boo.

"Hooooooooongh, sass!"

Embarrassed, I sat back in my seat. But perhaps something switched in the atmosphere, because after two more songs, the singing died down.

111

ALUTA

It took us four hours to get to Obo from Accra, and we were the second busload to arrive. I got off and carried my suitcase to the girls' dormitory close by.

We were in a secondary school, and I hurried to find a bed. Corners had always been the best places in all those years in boarding school. I tossed the narrow mattress over to its other side and proceeded to dust it down. Then I stretched my old white bedsheet to cover it.

Half an hour later, shouts from outside drew my attention to the fact that another bus had arrived. I went outside and watched as tired students tumbled out of it. Every now and then there were cries of recognition as old friends were reunited.

What were my chances of finding a good friend here? Sylvia lived at Kaneshie. Juaben lived at Labone Estates. And as for Mary, she lived all the way in Kumasi.

I was just about to return to the dormitory when I saw someone who looked familiar among the last of the travelers. It was in the way he walked with a bag slung over his shoulders.

"Banahene!" I screamed.

He turned and waved, and I ran towards him.

And just like that, my mood changed.

‹•›

On that first morning I was awakened by a bell — just like our days in boarding school. It took me some moments to recognize the bed and my surroundings. Next was the challenge of an ice-cold mountain shower in the bathhouse. Then I dressed in a pink T-shirt and old jeans.

There was no way I would risk my good clothes to evacuate cocoa, but I fluffed my curls out, outlined my eyes in kohl and brightened my lips with lipgloss.

Unlike the old colonial schools, Obo secondary school had no real character. It was painted white and green and looked like a dozen other recent schools with its low-cost construction. The administration block, dining hall and assembly hall were centrally placed between the girls' and boys' dormitories to keep them separate.

What was exciting was seeing Banahene in the dining hall. But there was little time to chat as we wolfed down Tom Brown — roasted corn porridge, along with a bun of sugarbread. Outside, the birds were singing and my canvas shoes were moist from the dew on the grass. And the air felt so fresh because we were high above sea level.

On the driveway were three boneshakers — our transportation to the cocoa-carrying station. These locally built trucks had half-open wooden bodies, and it took some athleticism to mount them by a high foothold on the side. I found a space on the middle bench of the first truck and squeezed between Banahene and my new friend Sharon. The diesel engine came to life — hoarse and throaty, and soon we were on the move.

As we weaved along the mountain road, we filled the boneshaker with our screams. The road was steep and narrow, and each time we rounded a bend I was sure we were going to fall over.

What if we had an accident? What if someone fell out? Our highways were so troubled by fatal car accidents, and I now understood why.

We spent that first morning at the carrying station waiting to get organized. There was always some person or some machine we had to wait for. My dad would have said, "Poor planning and poor maintenance — the bane of Ghanaian development!"

So we wasted the morning away. Then we had a snack of roasted plantain and groundnuts for lunch. Afterwards we weighed a few bags of cocoa and arranged them in a pile.

"Time is money," is nothing but a pathetic saying that no Ghanaian truly believes," said Banahene.

He was quite right, I thought. So many times I had been late for things and I never cared unless there was a punishment attached. Hanging around all day carrying this, weighing that in the middle of the Kwahu hills was so surreal that I had to pinch myself a couple of times just to be sure it was really happening.

What if this went on forever? I wondered. What a waste of time that would be.

The hours passed slowly. Then it was time to board the boneshakers back to our dormitories.

With the sun setting rapidly, we were soon plunged into darkness. Inside the truck, I listened to the rattling of our diesel engine as the vehicle shook violently all the way downhill. I couldn't see the depth of the valley. But I could imagine it, just by the incline of the truck and the harsh grating of the gears. I could smell the day's sweat and feel my heart against my ribs. The journey was worse in the night than it had been in the morning.

‹•›

That night there was an exchange between Banahene and Elias Dagadu in the dining hall. After the meal Dagadu introduced us to our camp leaders — four men and one woman who would help to run our programs — people to whom we could take our issues. Then he thanked us for our willingness to assist the beloved nation.

At our table, Sharon and one of her friends, Derek, burst out laughing. Banahene stood up when things quieted down.

"Elias Dagadu, why do you thank us for our willingness to assist with the cocoa project? Did we vote to come here?" Banahene had to shout his question as the hall was large.

"Can we, as good citizens, decline to help the country that pays our university tuition, when there is such a need?" said Dagadu.

"Mr. Dagadu, can you please answer my question? Do we have a choice to be here, or not?" demanded Banahene.

There was a buzz of voices from various tables. I saw the determination in Banahene's eyes. He was ready to argue for those of us who were angry at how we had been hustled out of school without so much as a vote.

"Historically, student representatives have always been chosen by voting. We don't even know how come you are our leader in this camp," said Banahene.

Somebody shouted, "I am more concerned about our meals than governmental thanks. What kind of meat was in that strange stew we just ate — bat or beef?"

The students roared with laughter. Dagadu waited until the laughter subsided.

"Someday you will be known for your patriotism in rescuing the nation at this time. Someday you will be feted for serving Mother Ghana," he said.

But Banahene turned to me and said, "Soon they will say that students voted unanimously to suspend their curriculum in support of the revolution. They will forget they forced us here. Just watch."

‹•›

The boneshakers showed up again the next morning, and I joined the others for the frightful uphill journey.

"You're back," said Derek mischievously, when I climbed in behind him.

"Scared but compliant," I said.

"She's a true Ghanaian. She complains and acquiesces," said Banahene.

"True. Our unspoken national motto is Me mpε me ho asεm — I don't want trouble!" said Sharon.

Indeed, it was hard to stand apart from everybody else. I knew what people would think if I continued to complain. "She thinks she's better than everyone." All our lives we had been taught to always fit in and never rock the boat. Girls, especially.

‹•›

It turned out that Banahene and I worked very well together, and I made up my mind that I would always work on his team. No matter how our leaders tried to organize the groups, I stuck close to him. If a leader tried to make me join another group, I simply broke orders and found Banahene again. He must have been quite flattered to

116

find me chasing him like that.

On a count of three, he would grab one end of a cocoa sack while I lifted the other end. Then we would haul it up a short distance to load on a truck. That small effort would take the wind out of me. And on the way back to the pile of cocoa, we would chat about this, that and the other. The time passed easily that way.

I loved the purity of mornings in Kwahu — the freshness of the mountain air and the coolness of the dew underfoot. I listened for the sound of the cock crowing every morning. But in the end, the hustle and bustle of our daily work dismissed the peace of the countryside.

There was a newspaper vendor near the entrance to the cocoa-carrying station, and Banahene bought two newspapers, the *Daily Crusade* and the *People's Daily Graphic*.

"How do you manage this every day?" I asked. I had never spent my money on a newspaper in all my life. It was something our parents did — people who worked a job and earned money.

"I used to buy just the *Graphic*, but these days I have to buy two papers. It's the only way to sift the real news from propaganda. If I could afford it, I'd buy about five papers daily," he said.

I observed the little details of Banahene's expressions as he skimmed through the first paper. I read in his eyes humor and cynicism and incredulity as he moved from one story to the next.

"Listen, Charlotte. Fifty soldiers from Kumasi's Fourth Battalion Infantry Brigade attacked a religious sect called The Lord Is My Shepherd. They killed the minister, dismembered his body and put his parts on public display," said Banahene.

"No way!" I said.

"Apparently it was just a small disagreement between a trigger-happy soldier and a policewoman who attended that church. And then everything got out of hand. You can't get deader than that," said Banahene, as he showed me the picture of a man lying dead on a street.

Sharon had just joined us beneath the shade tree in the yard.

"The soldiers are tripping!" she said.

"Power in the wrong hands," said Banahene. "They killed the policewoman, too."

"This can't be happening in Ghana," I said.

"Is the story in the *Daily Graphic*?" Sharon asked.

"No. It's in the privately owned *Crusade*. You have no idea what escapes the radar of journalism in our new socialist state," said Banahene wryly.

That night Banahene, Derek, Sharon and I gathered in an unlocked classroom. We spread dishes of kenkey and fish, which we had bought in the village, on two tables. We ate, relishing every mouthful.

"We always talk about things but isn't there something we can do?" asked Sharon. She was still appalled by the gory news we'd read earlier in the day.

We all agreed that it was time to stand up for what we believed in. I was quite clear that I did not believe in bloody military revolutions, and I certainly disagreed with a communist agenda for our nation. I just didn't know what standing up for something meant. I told them about our meetings in Dr. Ampem's office.

"You know, it was all talk! Every week, meet and talk," I said.

"Maybe for you it was talk but not for some of the others. The guy was recruiting comrades for the revolution. I've heard that he is one of the people behind this exercise," said Banahene.

"Well, let's do something right now," said Derek.

"So formed, the New Student Democrats. All say aye," I said.

There were four ayes, and Derek pulled a sheet of paper and a pencil out of his pocket and began to write.

"The New Student Democrats are hereby formed, and our vision is to affect student participation in the politics of the land," said Banahene grandly.

"We will work to help students in politics so long as they favor ideas of democracy," I said.

"Such ideas include advancing the rule of law, civil rights and human rights," said Sharon, as Derek wrote furiously to get it all down.

"We have a rough mission statement now, but we shall soon part ways. How will we carry on?" asked Derek.

"K.I.S.S. Keep It So Simple!" said Sharon. "Let's just plan to stand for positions in our Student Representative Councils."

"How about the National Union of Ghana Students — NUGS itself?" asked Derek.

"I'm not quite sure about personally standing for elections. But I can support the right candidates by joining their campaigns," I said.

"I'm going to stand for SRC secretary or treasurer at Cape Vars," said Sharon.

"I will campaign for you, Sharon," said Derek.

"I think Banahene should stand for SRC president. He would be amazing!" I said.

"Yes, you're the man for it, Banahene. You could even be the NUGS president," said Sharon. NUGS leadership is moving to UST this year."

"Maybe Charlotte should stand for NUGS president," said Banahene.

"Don't try to get out of this by making jokes," I replied.

"Seriously, Charlotte! Don't forget that Dr. Ampem saw something in you," said Banahene.

"Yeah, Charlotte, stand!" said Derek.

"Charlotte, how about this for a deal? If you stand for president, I will stand for secretary, and I will campaign for you," said Banahene.

"Yes, vote Charlotte for president! I don't think any of the universities have ever had a woman SRC or NUGS president," said Sharon.

"You sound like Dr. Ampem. But I can only promise that I will support Banahene's campaign for NUGS or SRC president," I said. "That, I can handle."

11

By the second week of the exercise, we were working shorter days because the drivers opted to drive us back while it was still daytime. Our leaders agreed that it was safer, and I was much happier.

It felt good to wash the sweat and dust off my body even if the water was so cold. After my shower, I went to find Banahene and we wandered into the small town on whose outskirts we were perched. We bought fried yam and pepper from the first vendor we saw. I loved the crispy corners of fried yam, cut in geometric shapes and well salted. Already the pepper sauce was soaking through the yam and I smacked my lips with pleasure.

What was it about street food that was so satisfying?

The fried yam vendor told us that a drum ensemble played for the locals every Friday evening. We walked around and saw the chief's house and two small churches, one Presbyterian and the other Roman Catholic. I wondered how Mass would sound in Twi. We passed by a school and some houses. A bank, a police station, a few commercial buildings and a row of kiosks made up the town center.

People greeted us affably and we responded. We strolled around until we got tired, then we headed back to the school. By this time the sun was just a reddish, purplish glow in the western sky, and we sat outside the assembly hall reminiscing.

"Do you remember how we met? asked Banahene.

"How could I forget? You knocked me over on the eighth-floor landing."

We both laughed.

"You should have taken my advice that day," said Banahene.

"I disagree. My subsequent ponding is a far better story to tell. Everyone gets such a laugh over it."

Banahene did not mention the one kiss between us. It was something he never referred to. And I didn't mention Asare and my passport.

It was strange how things had built up between Asare and me, only to fade over the first few weeks of the New Year because of the coup. Here I was now, in February, in the strangest place I could have imagined, high on the mountains of Kwahu, carrying cocoa bags by day and hanging out village style by night.

It was growing darker and mosquitoes were beginning to buzz and bite, so Banahene and I went walking to keep them at bay.

"I don't think I have ever seen a moon as brilliant as tonight's," said Banahene wistfully.

I looked up. The sky was flushed with moonlight, and the moon itself seemed so close.

Banahene placed his arm around my waist. He pulled me a little closer and tighter. We walked on, and the pepper sauce was still burning on my tongue. Then the talking stopped between us, and all I could hear was the sound of crickets screeching.

Suddenly, a chill passed through me, and I shivered.

"Cold?" he asked.

"No," I replied, even though the mountain air was cool.

But Banahene took off his cotton jacket and covered my shoulders. Then he drew me close towards him. All I could feel was the warmth of his breath on my face. Then his lips were on mine, and just like that, we were kissing.

After long moments his lips broke away from mine, but still he held on to me.

"I've wanted to do that ever since ... for a long time." He reached for my hand and pulled me along. We found an upstairs corridor in one of the classroom blocks. Leaning back against the wall, he drew me to him.

"Charlotte, I'm sure you know I am so attracted to you," he said.

"No," I mumbled. "I just know we really get along."

"Come on, Charlotte. Friends don't kiss like this."

"I didn't know what to make of that other kiss. You never mentioned it again," I said.

"I was up against ... against tremendous odds. I still am, I guess, except now I have you to myself. It's the one thing I can thank the socialists for," he said with a chuckle.

I laughed. "It hasn't been so bad after all, eh?"

123

"Charlotte, I might as well just say it. I am in love with you."

"It's probably the crazy moonlit night," I said.

"Maybe." He pulled me close again. His hands traveled over my back and my face, tracing lines of fire on my skin. We kissed again and again. Banahene pressed against me, and I felt every inch of him. I was surprised at how strong and taut he was, as the firm muscle of his thigh marked mine.

"It isn't just the moon, Charlotte," he whispered. "Be my girlfriend."

I didn't speak. It wasn't that I didn't love him, but there was still Asare, and I felt as though I owed him.

"Okay, baby, think about it for a while. But don't be too long thinking."

He brushed my hair with his hand, just where I cuddled against him. Banahene was tall, and my head felt snug just beneath his chin.

‹•›

Two weeks passed quickly as we bagged and loaded cocoa onto trucks. One Friday, a farmer visited us at the station. He had come to thank us for our work. A pleasant man, he brought fresh cocoa fruit to share with us.

I broke the yellow pod open with a machete, and inside were the pap-covered seeds. With my index finger I dislodged a seed and licked the gooey sweetness all around it.

Cocoa tasted good — tangy-sweet. But it wasn't sold fresh because it was the dried seeds that appealed to Caucasians, who then processed them for drinking as a beverage or as chocolate for dessert. This was where the money was hidden — inside the seed.

"Do you know about Tetteh Quarshie?" I asked the farmer.

"Who is he?" he asked.

"He is the famous Ghanaian blacksmith who first brought cocoa seeds into the country from Fernando Po island in 1876."

Every schoolchild learned this fact in history class. But this man was likely illiterate and perhaps had not gone to school beyond early primary.

"The Ga people have done something for Ghana," said the farmer.

I liked the modesty of rural folk. He explained that he had inherited his cocoa farm from his uncle. I asked him if his farm was nearby. But he laughed and said it was several hours away.

"I don't think you would know how to climb the slippery hills of Kwahu," he said with eyes twinkling. "Have you ever been to a farm before?"

"No," I said.

I was a city girl, only one generation removed from the farms of my people. I had never walked barefoot in mud and mire. I had never cut through thickets and creepers. I had never carried firewood on my head.

The farmer's name was Owusu Ansah. He was a typical Akan, smallish but strong. He was also very dark with discolored eyes. Sun and age did that to eyes, but he still had a twinkle in them.

"Have you ever had chocolate?" I asked.

"No," he said.

"What about Milo?" asked Banahene.

"Yes, I like that better than tea."

"Did you know Milo is made from cocoa?" asked Banahene.

"Do you think we village people know nothing at all?" he asked.

Suddenly, I wanted to give Mr. Owusu Ansah a gift. And I knew exactly what to do.

It took me twenty minutes to walk to the cluster of vendors we had passed on our way to the cocoa station. I purchased three bars of Golden Tree chocolate for the old man. I insisted he open one bar right there. I wanted him to taste it because I knew he would be more inclined to save the treat for his grandchildren.

He laughed as he ate a small piece of chocolate.

"This is too sweet for a man. I'll save it for the children," he said, wrapping the bar up again. He shook hands with the four of us, rearranged his cloth over his shoulders and left at a modest pace.

My grandfather had been a farmer, and my father had grown up helping him to grow cocoa. This would have been my life if my dad had not received a scholarship to study to become a secondary-school teacher.

I began to understand how privileged I was to be able to study at a tertiary institution, when I compared myself to those farmers who actually grew our cash crops. They worked the hardest to supply most of our country's foreign exchange, yet they didn't harvest those benefits of education, healthcare or even running water and electricity.

These were the things we talked about when our little group met in the evenings.

I loved the group, New Student Democrats. But I liked it better when Banahene and I escaped from the others to be a twosome. We would kiss until the whole world was nothing but a blur of sweet nerve endings — a fire in my belly.

For the first time, I truly recognized love. To think cocoa evacuation had made this possible!

<•>

In three weeks, students scattered all over the rainforest areas of Ghana accomplished all that it took to bring Ghana's cash crop to the ports. Dagadu announced on Wednesday that the following Friday would be the last day of our project at the Kwahu cocoa station.

The end was bittersweet. Sweet because we wanted to get back to school and bitter because we were leaving new friends behind. I had grown to love Sharon and Derek almost as much as my eighth-floor crew.

So, that Friday, four of us celebrated by going into Obo town to eat fufu and apɔnkye-kakra.

I could smell the chop bar from afar. I swallowed saliva in anticipation. There was no stronger flavor for soup than the meat of goats.

Afterwards we walked down to the town square, and the drum ensemble was playing Sikyi songs. There were six drummers in all, seated behind their drums playing with sticks or hands. There were two bell players as well.

The master drummer, who was dressed in a short smock, was standing with his drum on the slant. He beat the drum call with two crooks and sang in a bold tenor while the people echoed the song.

"Come on, let's dance," said Banahene. And he pulled me to the center of the clearing.

People cheered as they made way for us. They knew we were strangers. Banahene seemed to know what to do and so I followed his steps. Soon other dancers joined us.

After a while, Sharon and Derek left. A palm-wine seller arrived with the remains of the day's pot of wine. I sipped from Banahene's calabash. Then we walked back to the school, a little tipsy.

We made our way to our favorite place by the assembly hall. It was where Banahene had kissed me and told me he loved me.

Once more we were all alone and silence slipped between us. Banahene's hand came up on my shoulders and settled on the side of my neck. The hand trembled where it lay, and I held my breath for another moment.

I looked up at him and he smiled.

"We're leaving tomorrow, Charlotte. Will you be my girlfriend?"

"Yes," I whispered.

Then he bent his head and kissed me.

The next morning we were bused back to Accra along lonely roads to await the opening of our universities.

‹•›

Monday came, and it was great to be back in comfortable surroundings, even though I missed Banahene. My father, mother and I watched the TV in our living room. At seven o'clock, the national anthem played while the national coat of arms was displayed on our television sets. Then our thirty-four-year-old mulatto revolutionary head of state appeared behind a desk, dressed in his army fatigues, ready to read his speech.

In spite of my mother's reservations about the coup d'état, she found him handsome and rather liked his affected accent when he spoke English. These observations were met with scorn from my dad. I was only interested in what he had to say about the universities.

Soon enough, he congratulated the students, making it almost sound as if we had organized ourselves to go and rescue the cocoa export of the nation.

This time I didn't join my dad when he scoffed at our self-imposed leader. Cocoa evacuation had been more meaningful than I'd anticipated. Immediately after, as if to score points with the students, Rawlings announced the reopening of our universities on Friday. This meant that we would have an entire weekend to settle in.

"Hurray," I shouted, but my dad was unimpressed.

Poor Dad, our head of state irked him beyond what was reasonable. It was when I mentioned this that Dad confessed that he had taught him a long time ago at Achimota School. Dad said he had always been rebellious.

‹•›

Mama and I went to the market but there was only so much we could find. We bought a bag of gari, and some shrimp and dried pepper to make a bottle of shitor. In the past, our contacts at our local store helped us to buy a dozen tins of Ideal milk and a dozen tins of sardines. But in these days of revolution we were all too afraid to use our privileges. I ended up with only six tins of milk and four tins of sardines.

"Don't worry, Charlotte. I'll give you money to buy a crate of eggs. Eggs are good for protein," said Mama.

"See why I wanted you to go to Legon? You could have taken eggs straight from home," Dad complained.

"Go and see what the children of soldiers will have in their boxes. Nothing less than two dozen each of milk or sardines or even corned beef," said Mama bitterly.

"You're right. Revolutions simply turn our world on its head. Nothing much changes, except the few who benefit at the top," said my dad. "The rest of us have to suffer. This is what it means to be middle class — stuck."

Sometimes I felt sorry for Dad because he was so cynical. But I knew he had seen enough in the twenty-five years of our independence. It occurred to me that I might have been angry, too, if I was not deep in love.

12

On the eighth floor everyone had returned by Sunday night except for Sylvia. We heard that a couple of students had been sent abroad to school by their parents and would not be coming back. I wondered if Sylvia was one of them.

Banahene came to see me as soon as he arrived on campus. The days apart had made me miss him more than ever. My heart beat fast just at the thought of him. And whenever I actually saw him, my belly did complete somersaults. I was left breathless by the force of my feelings.

He brought newspapers for me to read. I copied his ways. I started my day listening to BBC's Voice of Africa. In the afternoon we tuned the radio to GBC 2, where we heard Ghanaian highlife songs, the news on the hour, and political rhetoric.

One night, after Banahene had left, I changed into my nightdress and got ready for bed. Mary was still up reading on the lower bunk when I returned my toothbrush to its holder. My mouth was tingly and I felt refreshed as Diana Ross and Lionel Richie sang the duet, "Endless Love." I placed one hand over my racing heart as I thought of Banahene's goodnight kiss.

"I have something to tell you," I said, sitting on Mary's bed.

"I can keep a secret," she replied.

"So long as you can tell Mr. Opoku, huh?" I joked.

"I don't tell Willie everything," she said defensively.

"Well, you can tell him this. Banahene is my boyfriend!"

"Charlotte, I knew that already. Anyone can tell by the way you have become so political — just like him. And you have this look in your eyes when he speaks, as if you're just waiting to eat his words. Even Willie knows, but he's sure Asare will come back and sweep you off your feet," said Mary.

"It's too late for that. I really love Banahene."

"Then he owes me, big time," said Mary with a laugh.

<•>

Our room was the womb of many conversations, perhaps because Mary was such a great cook. One afternoon she had me panting for her specialty — green plantain chips which she was frying on the balcony. I think the entire floor could smell it. I knew it was meant for Mr. Opoku, and so I was very glad when she decided to share the delicacy.

Banahene, Juaben and I were eating the chips with peanuts while the news blasted away on the radio. The news included a clip of Flight Lieutenant Rawlings' speech.

We listened as his voice was drowned by the cheers of his fans as he tried to speak Twi.

Mary said, "Oh, Ghanaians! They don't even care what is being said. They're so impressed by an oburoni speaking Twi."

"It's his wishy-washy not-British-not-American accent that impresses people. All he has to do is keep them entertained with the usual divisive arguments — turning one group against the other," I said.

"It's really hard to understand the mystery of this man. It's not just his accent, though. People are caught up in his personality. He has charisma," said Juaben.

"Do you think J.J.'s fame rides on an artifact of imperialism — fair skin?" asked Banahene.

"With so much blood on his hands, I don't know why people should care about his color, accent or charisma," said Mary.

"Those things always matter," said Banahene.

"It's the truth that matters. It isn't educated people who have run the country down. It is inept politicians and greedy leaders, and for the most part they have been soldiers," said Mary.

"Don't let the Ghanaian intelligentsia off so easily. They have looked out only for themselves. Nobody looks out for the poor. Don't blame the poor now that they have power on their side. That's what happens when a country allows education to open up a huge class gap between the haves and have-nots," said Banahene.

I loved these discussions, especially when we could laugh about some things and enjoy Mary's delicious offerings at the same time. I felt like I had grown so much in a short time. I knew what I liked and didn't like in a government.

Mary served us her homemade pineapple-ginger drink. Juaben sipped hers like a lady, but I could barely set mine down between sips.

As for Banahene, he drained the juice down to the dregs and let out a soft burp.

"Excuse you," I said, somewhat embarrassed.

"To *air* is human," said Banahene.

"What?" I said.

"That's what my semi-literate uncle says whenever he lets out a giant burp."

"Uncle is full of malapropisms," said Mary, as she re-filled our glasses.

It was good to be back in school.

‹•›

Dr. Ampem did not surface during that first week of school, and someone said a new lecturer would start with us on Thursday.

Sylvia finally arrived on Sunday afternoon, but all we saw of her were the boxes she dropped off. I connected with her at the English lecture the next day. Afterwards, Juaben, Sylvia and I walked back to the hall together.

I asked Sylvia where she had been overnight. Her answer was nothing more than a giggle, and Juaben whispered, "Awɔɔshia!"

We let the matter rest. Love was a private thing.

There was something different about Sylvia. It wasn't

her new clothes or hairstyle of woven cornrows. Her makeup was much louder, and when she spoke she waved her hands as though she was in charge of everyone.

It soon became clear to us that her sympathies now lay completely with the government.

"Doesn't it feel good to do a selfless act for the benefit of everyone? We're better people for it."

"What selfless act?" I asked.

"The cocoa project. We have earned much foreign exchange for the country already. This government will make a real difference. Ghana will be saved," said Sylvia.

"Saved?" I said.

And she merely shrugged her shoulders when I asked what she thought about the killing of the policewoman and the pastor in Kumasi.

Sylvia had changed.

"These people have held power before under a different name, and they murdered people. Some people I know lost their fathers to firing-squad bullets," I said.

"Charlotte, you have to separate the former revolution from this one. Even then, it was the fervor of revolution that brought on the excesses, and there was very little Rawlings could do about it," she said.

"Propaganda shit! He is the one who wrote the word accountability in blood. They held all our former leaders responsible for the financial losses that had occurred under their watch. They killed them. And now he wishes to pass the buck on to his soldiers?"

Sylvia avoided my eyes. "The thing is this. We have a chance now to help build up a fallen nation. We should try to let bygones be bygones."

"A leopard never changes its spots, and Ghanaians will never forget the killings of the 1979 coup. Ghanaians may be silent now because they are afraid, but they can see the same abuses emerging even now," I said.

"Sylvia, where did you go for the cocoa exercise?" asked Juaben, and I knew she was trying to reset the conversation.

"I was in Accra," she said.

"Accra? Were you hiding there, or what?" I asked incredulously.

"No. I was attached to head office," Sylvia replied.

"Where is head office?" I had never heard of a head office for the cocoa exercise.

"The National Service Secretariat," said Sylvia.

"What did you do there?" I asked.

"A group of us coordinated the program. We also did evaluations," said Sylvia.

"I don't get it. So while the rest of us were sweating it out, you lived a cushy life in Accra?" I asked.

"It wasn't cushy. We even traveled to parts of the Eastern Region to check on the work," said Sylvia defensively.

"And how did you get selected?" I asked.

"Mensah told me they were looking for people to run the operations. He asked me if I was interested," said Sylvia.

"I suppose Mensah also worked from headquarters. Maybe he was the boss," I said sarcastically.

"What's your problem?" Sylvia retorted angrily.

"You people disgust me. You go on and on about laboring with the common man. And at the very first instance of real work, you go and find cushy jobs doing nothing. You can tell Mensah I said that."

"What about you, Charlotte? Aren't you blindly following Banahene? You used to be Dr. Ampem's protégé. What happened to you?" said Sylvia, and she stomped off angrily.

I took Juaben's hand to prevent her from rushing after Sylvia.

"Don't mind her. Banahene was right about their lies. Already newspapers have reported that students voted to go out and recover the cocoa. They are using our compliance as a show of support for the government. Worse still, they refer to the cocoa exercise as an example of their capacity to get things done. Aah!" I said.

"I don't like this at all," said Juaben. "I have relatives who used to be very close. Now they are at loggerheads because one family supports the new government, whereas the other family suffered at the hands of the former AFRC."

"Disagreements are not a bad thing, you know. It's better than being quiet and swallowing what you dislike. Sylvia is not my enemy, but I won't pretend to agree with her just to be friends. My only regret is taking her to Dr. Ampem's meetings. It is the reason she met Mensah, and why she has turned into one of them," I said.

"Don't blame yourself, Charlotte. Sylvia is not the only one who has changed. Love is a strange animal. You should know that."

⟨•⟩

The next couple of days were very hot. On Wednesday afternoon I walked back to the hall with Banahene after lectures. We said goodbye in the lobby. All I wanted was my bed and a nap. I went upstairs, tied back the curtains and opened the louvers to let in as much air as possible. I wished I could have opened the door, but that would have been the end of privacy and a restful sleep. I had stripped down to a skimpy tube top and shorts while I blasted the table-top fan at full speed. I lay there on top of my covers with my eyes closed.

A shadow fell across my window. A moment later there was a tentative knock on my door. I slipped off my bed and opened the door.

At the door stood a man I had never met before. Simply dressed in a light brown political suit, he was slight with graying hair and a small moustache. I thought he was possibly lost.

"Good afternoon, miss. Are you Charlotte Adom?" he asked. I nodded in surprise.

"I am Samuel Duah, Asare's cousin," he said as he extended his hand and shook mine.

After my initial surprise, I remembered my manners and asked the man in.

Suddenly I was embarrassed to be in my tube top and shorts. It was too much skin in a tiny space with a stranger.

Mr. Duah sat down in our armchair. I offered him a drink of water, and then I sat by the desk. He opened his bag and pulled out a letter. He said that Asare had instructed him to deliver the letter to me personally.

"How is Asare?" I asked.

"He is well," said Mr. Duah, and a little smile played at his lips.

I took the letter and opened it. Inside it was some money in pounds sterling. But there was also a note. I read it quickly, recognizing Asare's fine cursive.

My darling Charlotte,
Life itself has turned upon its head and I am still trying
to pick myself up. It isn't safe for me to return to Ghana
as most of my colleagues in the petroleum business have
either been harassed or confined. It is very hard for me to
manage my affairs from here, but I am making the most of
it by way of trusted friends and family, such as Samuel. I
wanted you to meet him. I wanted someone in my family
to know about you and my intentions for you. I want you
to have someone who can help you if ever you are in need.
Samuel isn't just my cousin. He also knows much about
my business. You are in my mind and in my heart so don't
let me go. Don't forget me. I would like you to visit me dur-
ing the holidays, now that you have a passport. Samuel
can help you make the necessary arrangements. Here's a
small sum of money to enjoy. Please accept it. And do write
to me.
Love always,
Asare.

I finished reading the note, folded it carefully and returned it to the envelope. I knew I'd read it again.

"Mr. Samuel Duah, thank you for bringing me this letter.
Asare sent me some money but I am afraid I can't accept
it. I would like to give that back to you, please."

"Oh, no, sister. Don't do that. The money is nothing, just
Asare's gift to a friend. I can't accept it, either, so please
don't embarrass me by returning it. I won't know what to
say to Asare. And he did not inform me about money."

I realized I had embarrassed us both and apologized. I
asked Samuel if he knew Mr. William Opoku.

"I know Willie very well," he said. "You can send a message to me through him, if you need anything. My wife and I live in Oforikrom. You can come for lunch at our home anytime."

I wasn't interested in starting up with Asare again, but I wanted things to go well for him. Why was he shrouded in so much mystery? But Samuel Duah was guarded.

"This government is giving us some problems but time will tell," he said. "We have seen such things before. It may blow over before long. However, if you wish to write a reply to Asare, I can post it for you. I shall be happy to do that."

13

I knew about field hockey from secondary school. In the first year we had studied game rules from a book. For the next four years, we practiced the skills of hitting, dribbling and pushing during gym period. I had even played for a term on my junior house team.

And so I agreed to try out for the women's team Banahene was coaching.

I hadn't run since June when my A-Level exams were done, and I was out of shape. My heart was pounding in my ears as I practiced passing on the run. My T-shirt clung to my back and I felt giddy from the heat.

After the practice, we stopped at Republic Hall for a 7 Up — Banahene's treat.

The man at the till knew Banahene. "Dr. Ampem has been made the new minister for education. It was announced this afternoon," he said.

"We have friends in high places," said Banahene, winking at me.

"I wonder what he's going to do. Maybe he will abolish private elementary schools or extend free education to cover every child in every region, not just the Northern and Upper Regions. That would be something," I said.

I had dropped out of Ampem's group since our return from the cocoa exercise, but I still remembered the debates we'd had on education.

"Do you think he's still in touch with Mensah and the others?" I asked.

Banahene shrugged. "Ask Sylvia."

But Sylvia no longer talked to me about their meetings. In fact, she hardly spoke to me at all and never came to my room.

"Sharon wrote to me," I said, fishing for the letter in my bag. "Derek is standing for the position of hall representative. She wants to know if any of us would contest for the NUGS leadership."

"Not the NUGS. This is the first time we are seeking office," said Banahene.

"SRC, then?" I asked.

"I think so," said Banahene. "It should be easier for us to represent students in our own university rather than students all over the nation."

"It still won't be easy," I said. "Apparently campus socialists are very tight with the government. There are rumors about trips to Accra to consult with members of the government."

"No smoke without fire, Charlotte. I can easily imagine Mensah and Sylvia calling on Dr. Ampem at the ministry of education. I bet you can, too."

He put his glass to his lips and didn't stop until he had swallowed the last fizzy drop of soda.

‹•›

Mr. Opoku brought Mary and me fried rice and chicken from Score Board, a restaurant at the stadium. It was only after we had finished it all off that he talked about Asare.

"I have his address if you want to write to him," he said.

I had been procrastinating — unwilling to tell Asare to forget about me as I was in a relationship with Banahene. Asare had suffered many losses and I didn't want to add to them, especially as he had been so generous to me.

Later that night, I forced myself to write. It was hard to find the words.

Dear Asare,
I have been quite concerned for you. Therefore I was very glad when you sent me a note through Mr. Samuel Duah. I would like to thank you for the passport as well as the air ticket you gave me for my trip to Accra for the Christmas break. You are very generous. I hope things will calm down soon, so you can come home peacefully. I'm not sure what the challenges are but I hope you can overcome them. We're all looking for a better Ghana.
I also wanted to let you know that I have a boyfriend now. I am sorry things didn't work out for us. However, I

would like us to remain friends. And if there is something I
can do for you, please don't hesitate to ask.
Take care,
Charlotte
P.S. Thank you for the money.

I folded the letter into an envelope. I would post it the next day at the university plaza. I knew there would be no free tickets to England or anywhere else. But it didn't matter. My heart only wanted Banahene.

⟨•⟩

Banahene's friend was standing for NUGS president. To gain experience, Banahene and I volunteered to help him. I also roped in Jordan. We pinned posters on notice boards that said, *Get involved! It is your life.*

As the weeks went by, I became bolder and knocked on all the doors in Africa Hall to plead for votes. I got into many discussions and I learned about the power of university students. Most of us were single with no dependents. We were also smart enough to know what we wanted, and passionate enough to demand it.

We watched our candidates sweep the elections to become the new NUGS representatives. My first taste of political victory felt like walking on air.

Banahene called a meeting at Queen's cafeteria. It was a few minutes after seven when I got there. Three bottles of Supermalt were sweating on the table, and Banahene and Jordan were deep in conversation.

Banahene opened my bottle and dropped in a straw. I drew a long mouthful.

"Guys, I'm writing to tell Sharon and Derek what we have accomplished with NUGS," I said.

"Tell Sharon and Derek that *we* are going to stand for the SRC leadership," said Banahene.

"Banahene will stand for president," said Jordan. "He is the most experienced. What do you prefer, Charlotte, secretary or treasurer?"

"I don't want to contest as a candidate," I said.

"You're popular, Charlotte. You understand the issues and you speak well," said Banahene.

"Come on, Charlotte. We can't do it without you. You are the inspiration for women, especially," said Jordan.

"I have to think about it," I said. I could imagine my dad's displeasure. He wouldn't want me involved in anything other than my studies.

"You know you can do this, Charlotte," said Banahene.

"Say yes, Charlotte. Join our ticket. Help us win," said Jordan.

"Okay," I said at last.

‹•›

We began to plan a campaign right away. There was some way to go before the SRC elections, and we could only hope that the momentum we had attained during the NUGS campaign would hold out for us.

We established our base at Republic Hall. Someone had started selling chocolate-ice there and Banahene and I loved them. Chocolate also reminded me of the farmer we had met at Obo during the cocoa exercise.

I sat in Banahene's room, sucking hard on the narrow piece of plastic which contained the icy treat. And I was careful not to dribble chocolate on my shirt, from the leaks which appeared spontaneously in the poorly manufactured plastic.

Banahene waved an envelope at me.

"My dad wrote something curious in his last letter, and it has got me thinking," he said.

I never wrote home, and I marveled that Banahene could discuss his activism with his parents. I kept my parents in the dark about my activities in student politics. It was simpler that way. I knew my dad would say, "Charlotte, you are at that university to get a degree. So mind your own business, and stop playing politics."

"What did your dad say?" I asked.

"You are not as invincible as you think," Banahene read aloud.

"What do you think he means?" I asked.

"I guess he means we could still lose even with the momentum in our favor," Banahene replied.

"He just doesn't want you to take things for granted. We've got to work till we get past the post," I said.

Banahene made much of the fact that the decision to send us out to evacuate cocoa had never been put to the vote — not that most students would have attended an SRC meeting either way. Still, the lie irked, along with the sense that we had been controlled by other students in collusion with the rebel government.

‹•›

I could sense the increase in momentum as we entered the last week of the campaign. Even my lecturers knew I was standing for elections. And people I didn't know would stop on campus to encourage me.

I did not know what to do about being so visible. On the one hand it was terribly exciting, but it also made me feel vulnerable.

We were counting heavily on Jordan to bring us the Christian Fellowship vote. For the campaign, I found my rosary and discovered the Catholic church on campus. I soaked in the sweetness of the gentle Sunday homily.

A few days before the vote, I went with Juaben to a prayer meeting. There I received prayer for success in the elections. Prayer by such a large congregation was very comforting. These prayers were drenched in scripture, voiced out loudly and convincingly with exuberant cries of Amen. Juaben said the people praying were prayer warriors — an apt name, I thought.

"You're going to win. I saw it in a vision," Juaben said afterwards. And her eyes were shining. She said it was her very first vision.

14

I had gone through my speech at least ten times for the SRC manifesto night. There were even portions I had memorized. I felt good reading it out loud, pausing at the right places to hit my punch lines.

This was the night to seal the campaign. Voting was scheduled for the next day.

Backstage, I listened first to Banahene and then to Jordan as they rehearsed their speeches. We had arrived early enough to see our opposition as they came in. They were all guys and everyone was well dressed, favoring white shirts and dark pants. Only one man wore his Batakari and rubber tire shoes with pride. Banahene had on a red, yellow and green tie to represent Ghana.

"You're a fine gentleman," I said, straightening the knot on his tie.

"I was thinking of wearing a bow tie and a three-piece suit," he said with a grin.

Mensah came in with Sylvia. It seemed as though Sylvia

148

would walk right past, as she avoided eye contact with me. But I was feeling quite pumped so I said hello too loudly to be ignored.

"Hi," Sylvia muttered. But Mensah shook hands with us.

"She's the moral support," I whispered to Banahene.

"You're more powerful," he said.

Mensah looked more imposing with his height and wide shoulders. But he could not match Banahene's baby-faced charm. Mensah was too quarrelsome to be charming. Still, he was formidable in his own way.

Noises from the auditorium told me the Great Hall was filling fast, and I calmed myself down with slow steady breaths. It was best to relax before the competition, before one let loose on a charge of adrenaline.

Our strength lay in the unity of our team — all for one and one for all, just like the Three Musketeers. Instead of running individual campaigns, we had been able to share our strengths. Each of us had roped in friends, floormates and even the friends of friends. Our hope was that if one of us could get a voter onside, then the others would be assured of that voter's vote. One of our slogans was "Unity is strength!" As a unit we could change university life for the better, and change the nation, too.

"Tonight is about guarding our support and convincing undecided voters. We may even steal some socialists to our side. I think we're ready," said Banahene.

The buzz in the large hall dissipated as we were ushered in. There were eight of us competing for three offices. I glanced at our opponents as we took our seats on the stage. Mensah reminded me of a crouching lion — composed and yet tense.

All eyes were on the outgoing SRC president as he began to address the audience. In just a few minutes he described the order we were to approach the podium to deliver our speeches. A spattering of applause welcomed the first candidate who was standing for the position of treasurer, and then we were on a roll.

I tried hard to listen to what each candidate was saying. I clapped politely after each turn at the microphone. I hoped my supporters were listening hard. I had designated certain members of my team to make notes when my competition spoke, so they could frame questions to destabilize them. There was something in me that liked this kind of intellectual wickedness. It was part of my strategy.

I was the fourth to go, and the only woman to speak. I wavered between pride and nervousness. I had on the blue dress with yellow flowers that I had worn for matriculation, but this time there were no flowers in my hair.

"When you're seeking votes, you should be stylish without being too fabulous. You should look smart and not vain," Mary had said when I piled on the accessories.

So I took off the bangles and changed my funky bead necklace for a small chain. I wanted to attract both guys and ladies to my side.

By the time I was done with my speech, I was perspiring on my nose and forehead with the stress of it all. I could have sworn that I had received the best applause, though.

Then it was Mensah's turn. And his fans gave him very loud cheers. In return, he gave the power salute, which made the crowd roar. Mensah knew how to play the game, and he spoke confidently.

"My fellow students, I know your needs. I have the

know-how to be your president. I will work with the administration for an enriching student experience. And we shall work with the government for a better Ghana. Together we can do this. So tomorrow exercise your best choice and vote for me."

When he raised the issue of our allowance, the audience yelled his nickname, Bangla Mensah, and the hall thundered with the cheering.

Could Banahene top that?

Banahene was the last to speak. He spoke clearly and passionately.

"If I win, I promise to represent you and not speak for you. I promise to open up SRC meetings and encourage discussions and the vote. I will respect your opinion on matters relating to our campus as well as the country. I can promise that you will not wake up one morning and find yourselves working on a railroad in Tarkwa, wondering how you got there!"

I could tell Banahene had captured the hearts of the students, even if Mensah was more charismatic. Certainly all of Africa Hall was in support of him. Women loved a handsome man.

The moderator opened for questions from the audience. To my surprise, several of the questions came to me, and I answered them to thunderous applause. I was amazed at how much I enjoyed the limelight, and even more the butting of wits. In a way it reminded me of the debates I had with my dad.

Then the president announced the final round of questions from the floor, and I could not believe the night was nearly over.

From the back, a man walked right down the center aisle and up to the podium. His heels clicked deliberately against the terrazzo floor. He was wearing a light blue T-shirt over blue jeans, and he had a jaunty strut to his walk.

He took his time to set up his question, fiddling with the microphone and clearing his throat. His was the last question, and he directed it to me.

"Madam Charlotte, can you as a lady represent real student needs? You see, I have it from reliable sources that you have a rich businessman boyfriend who supports you. Are you going to help us all to find the same kind of benevolence, or do you have real solutions for students?"

I was too shocked to answer, and then a grand swell of protest arose from the floor — the same booing that I had endured on the bus to Kwahu. It took the moderator a few minutes to calm the assembly down. He said the question was in poor taste and was to be disregarded.

But it was too late.

I tried to act confidently while the moderator summed the evening up with final words of thanks. Then I hung around with our supporters until the last of them left. I could only hope that my smile looked genuine as I received congratulations. Jordan took off to his hall, and I was left with Banahene.

I deflated like a punctured car tire. All I wanted was to go and hide. Banahene put an arm around me and drew me close.

"I feel so humiliated," I said, catching a sob before it formed.

"You did well, Charlotte. I think you did the best of us all. Perhaps you should have stood for president," said Banahene as we walked back from the Great Hall.

"Don't lie, Banahene."

"Politics is dirty, and that guy is one of those who hits below the belt. I think most people would realize that he was just a mischief-maker. Don't let him get to you," said Banahene.

But I wondered if Banahene was thinking about Asare and me.

Gloom, like a blanket, wrapped itself around me. In the end, we just hugged each other when we parted. We didn't kiss. I wasn't feeling that way.

15

"Charlotte, today is your big day. Get up, get up, get up! The entire floor is going with you down the stairs, and we're going to make noise all the way to the ballot boxes," said Mary.

I wiped the sleep from my eyes. The day had indeed come, but I hadn't expected my floormates to make a fuss about it. Mary had always been especially cool about the election. But here she was now, very excited.

"What's the plan?" I asked, stretching down to the tips of my toes.

"We're marching down at 9 a.m. to vote. Wear this red shirt and jeans," she said, giving me her own T-shirt.

Promptly at 8:55, Juaben came to get us. All the eighth-floor girls were ready with a loud cheer as I stepped out of my room. Everyone was there except Sylvia, and they were all in red T-shirts.

A rush of excitement hit me as one of my neighbors began a popular athletics cheering song.

"On my way, I will remember Charlotte."

Singing the echo, we went downstairs, drawing more people to join our party. The cheering got louder when I cast my vote. Then we went off, a happy group to breakfast.

By ten o'clock I was seated among my friends, swallowing mouthfuls of Hausa koko and munching on sugarbread. People came over just to say hello or give me a high five. Emily, my old schoolmate, came down with her roommate and joined us.

"Do you remember that first night here when we met at the dining hall?" she asked.

I nodded. I had been so anxious about roommates, fitting in and just getting along in university.

"Look at you now," she said. And there was admiration in her eyes.

‹•›

Africa Hall votes were counted in our common room at 6 p.m. The electoral commissioner of Africa Hall then announced the results by bush telephone from the lower roof. I made my way to the Great Hall with my friends, but none of them could take my anxiety away. As I was the only contestant from Africa Hall, it wasn't surprising that I'd won there. But what about the other halls full of men?

Everything was going so fast. Mary made jokes. Juaben squeezed my hand and gave me hugs, but all I felt was my heart beating frantically.

In every hall they were counting votes. Then we would all meet at the Great Hall for the tally at 8 p.m. What if I lost? What if I was the only one to lose in our team? What if our team lost in the end? My world was in a tailspin.

I could hear groups of people singing victory songs in the darkness.

"Don't worry. You're going to win," said Mary.

I realized in that moment that I could survive anything with the support of my friends.

I made my way to the front of the hall where Jordan was standing quietly beside Banahene. The other contestants were huddling there in groups — everyone with bated breath, waiting.

The sound system crackled and came alive. The SRC electoral commissioner was ready to announce the results. I held my breath until I heard Jordan's name and tally. He won by a mile.

Moments later, my numbers were called. It was close but I had won. I might have fainted if Banahene hadn't held me.

At last, Banahene's name was announced as the president. He had beaten Mensah by three hundred votes.

With a shout, he pumped his fist upwards. Yes!

People were cheering wildly, crowding us. Banahene's contest had been the fiercest, yet here we were, all three of us in victory.

People started shouting, "Speech, speech!"

Somehow we made it to the stage. Gathering around the podium, Banahene gave his acceptance address. It was gracious and full of sincerity, extending gratitude to include even his opponents.

Jordan thanked the voters in his speech. We hugged each other and raised our hands in the victory sign.

Then it was time to give my speech. But nobody would listen because they were too happy to be quiet. And we were the focus of this wild jubilation. In a flash I caught a glimpse of power, and why people held on to it as if it was their own possession. It felt good to bask in the adoration of one's peers.

Perhaps this was why Rawlings and his cohort had returned themselves to power.

Then the crowd, as one, picked up Banahene and raised him shoulder high. Singing at the top of our voices, we left the Great Hall for Republic Hall, where Banahene had to give another speech.

He was only in the middle of it when a group of six guys charged the podium. The crowd began to cheer. They carried Banahene to the pond in the center of the courtyard and dropped him in, unceremoniously, to swim with the fish.

It was my turn to laugh as he climbed out soaked to the bone.

"We're even," I said, as he dripped all the way up the stairs to his room.

‹•›

The vice chancellor invited us to tea the day after our victory. As Banahene, Jordan and I sat on his plush settee, sipping tea from dainty china cups, our VC shared his expectations.

"Your most important duty is to keep me informed of student needs. Work with me, and I promise to lend a listening ear. Don't stir up the students to discontent.

Remember, the military is in charge so don't get carried away. Another unscheduled break will jeopardize the school year."

"Yes, sir," we chorused.

I couldn't help thinking of my dad as he said in parting, "Do not forget that your first priority is to get good degrees. Student leadership is for a year but a degree is for a lifetime. Time slips away like sand in the hand."

Our office was very different from the vice chancellor's. I looked around me. The old SRC executives had left the room tidy but the walls were in need of paint. There was an old yellow curtain hanging over the only window, and a dirty white fan stood in the corner beside a banged-up filing cabinet.

Banahene took the old swivel chair behind the desk. I took the wooden chair by the file cabinet and Jordan sat on the chair opposite Banahene.

"Here's to the new improved SRC," I said.

Jordan gave me a high five. Then he touched fists with Banahene in a macho salute.

"We will be the best SRC this university has ever had," he said.

The night before, Banahene and I had talked about our roles in the SRC and especially about how we would manage our love for each other.

"We're going to have to be very professional with SRC business," he'd said.

I agreed. That meant no touching during meetings.

"Now what?" I asked.

"Our first meeting begins. The secretary takes minutes," said Banahene.

So I wrote as the others spoke.

Our priorities included a definition of our executive vision, the organization of our financial papers and plans for maintaining student engagement.

"Don't write this down, Charlotte," said Banhene in a quieter voice. "I've been contacted by leaders of the Ghana Bar Association and the Ghana National Association of Teachers. They would like to work with us."

"Add to that the Christian Council. I have also been contacted by a leading independent pastor in Kumasi," said Jordan.

Nobody had contacted me.

"I think we should be careful of agenda other than our own. We do not want to be played as pawns by other interests," I said.

"But we did say to our fellow students that we would stand for democracy in Ghana. If we're to be effective we shall have to work with other like-minded groups," said Banahene.

"So long as we do things our way," I insisted.

⟨•⟩

We called it a new era, but our meetings were hardly different from past meetings. There were more people in attendance, but they continued to complain about mundane things like dining-hall food, allowances, student loans and running water. Juaben and Mary came to the meetings for my sake.

Mensah was now too dignified to make brash arguments about bangla, but others had taken his place while he became a general critic of all our executive decisions. He sometimes sat with Sylvia in the front row where he could easily interrupt the meeting.

In some ways student politics was disappointing, but I learned that one had to plow through boring issues to get to the vision. We had promised to keep the students well informed and to seek their votes on matters that concerned them. We had also promised accountability, transparency and trust.

"I thought we were going to change the world. Instead it's one stupid motion after another," I said to Banahene and Jordan after a particularly annoying meeting.

"There will always be those who are stuck on feeding allowances," said Jordan, amused.

"These people are the ones who will keep us on our toes," said Banahene.

I stifled a sigh.

⟨•⟩

Even if student politics was boring, my relationship with Banahene was blossoming. I had made the cut on the hockey team. I was feeling healthier than ever. Mary and Mr. Opoku were making plans for their marriage by Akan traditional custom in August. They would save the church wedding until next year. Jordan seemed to be interested in Juaben, but he hadn't yet stirred up the courage to ask her out formally.

I got a letter from Sharon. She had won her bid to become the SRC treasurer at Cape Coast University. I couldn't wait to meet up with her during the holidays.

I felt like I had everything — love, friends and influence.

June was hurrying towards July, and it started to get intense with course work. Essays were due. Between my social life and the SRC, I tried to remember that I was in school to get a degree.

I searched through my photo album and found a picture of my dad. He was smiling. I peeled the photo off the sticky page and pinned it on my notice board. Then I found a piece of paper and a red marker. I wrote words I could imagine him speaking: "Charlotte, you have been sent to university purposefully to get a degree. Don't forget that!"

Even if he wasn't the carrot, my dad was the helpful end of the stick.

Our visitors laughed whenever they saw the note, but it worked for me. It probably worked for them, too.

I spent an entire evening writing a paper on the Bond of 1844. The only references I could find for my work could not be checked out of the library. So I had to sit there, chewing the end of my pencil and making copious notes. There was much to read, and I forgot the time until the night librarian said the library was closing.

I packed my books immediately. At that time of the night the library road was deserted.

In the distance, I saw the lights of a car come on, and then the car began to move up the road.

Suddenly it was upon me. I jumped off the road and landed on my bottom. The car screeched past. It was a Pajero.

I picked myself up and brushed the dirt off my clothes. My heart was thumping in my chest. Even if I had strayed onto the road, the driver could have honked his horn instead of driving me into the bushes.

I thought of Banahene when I saw the Republic Hall lights. I would tell him about my narrow escape tomorrow. I crossed the road to connect with the Africa Hall driveway. The road was very dark.

I had only gone a few feet on the driveway when I was suddenly bathed in light. A car came to life with a cough. As I drew close to it I realized it was a Pajero. A window came down and I saw a man with a black cap pulled down low over his forehead.

Even in the darkness he wore dark glasses.

He said, "Charlotte Adom, be very careful. The revolution will not tolerate upstarts like you."

I ran all the way to the hall.

16

That same night, June 30th, 1982, while I was sleeping, three high court judges and one army officer were kidnapped from their homes. Shockwaves rattled the entire country as we discussed what might be the advent of a reign of terror. I could imagine my dad saying, "Oyiwa — agenda exposed!"

We were now face to face with the underlying anxiety that I had sensed in my parents and their friends on the night of the coup d'état.

There was an outcry led by the Ghana Bar Association. Not even the fear of the military could tone them down. That evening, Banahene summoned Jordan and me to a meeting. It turned out that he had received an invitation for our SRC to attend a meeting in town. Fear raised goosebumps on my skin.

We took a taxi to Amakom. Then we took another one which wound us through the neighborhood roads.

Getting off beside a school, we walked the rest of the way to the house of the Anglican bishop of Kumasi. That was how cautious we were.

A young man ushered us into a large square room furnished with four overstuffed armchairs and two large sofas. I followed the pattern of Adinkra symbols on the upholstery. There was the ram's horn for strength, the two-headed crocodile for unity in diversity and the Adinkrahene — the coil that represented the unknowable God in life and nature.

Two men in suits stood in one corner of the room talking. A third man dressed in a minister's collar was seated by the window.

The doorbell rang again. It was the NUGS president and secretary from our university. I wondered if they had chosen a roundabout way to arrive as we had.

Just then, the bishop came in. He was casually dressed in an African print shirt and black trousers.

"Hello," he said, as he went around the room shaking hands.

He was a small man with a seemingly mild manner. His eyes smiled at the corners — kind eyes in a powerful man.

"Sit down, please," he said, pointing us to the seats. We introduced ourselves to each other. The two men who had been deep in conversation were lawyers.

Mr. Tevie was more vocal than the other lawyer. He explained that one of the kidnapped judges was connected with lawsuits regarding divestitures of certain state-owned properties. The other two had reversed judgments passed by the makeshift courts of the former AFRC government. The bar association now had people searching the records to discover all they could about those cases. Everyone feared the worst for the judges.

"The lady justice was a breastfeeding mother," Mr. Tevie whispered. And the bishop covered his mouth with one hand as if to stop a groan.

My tears came unbidden and I brushed them away. I'd heard her name mentioned more than once at home. My mother would remind us that Justice Cecilia Koranteng-Addow was her schoolmate. She'd held her up like a role model, hoping that I would choose that same path someday. Women high court judges in Ghana could be counted on one hand. She was a national treasure.

"If we keep silent, this may become the beginning of an unprecedented bloodbath," said the bishop.

"We have a moral duty to speak up," said the other lawyer. He was the president of the Kumasi chapter of the Ghana Bar Association.

"What do you think?" said the bishop. His eyes roamed the room.

"The country is perched right on the brink of disaster. It may be up to us to save it," said the NUGS president.

Banahene and Jordan did not say anything. We were new to this kind of thing.

Finally the bishop said, "In times like these the strength of our nation rests with you, our young brothers and sisters. We will need you to rise up and protest the evil that has been born. Be assured that we shall support you."

I wasn't going to jump into things just because the bishop said so. We would return to our campus to discuss the issue, for each of us had responsibilities towards those we represented.

For the next week, I made a daily pilgrimage to the library, where I scoured all the newspapers on display. Most of them merely repeated the press releases from the Ghana News Agency. But whatever was lacking in the printed news was replenished by the grapevine. All eyes were on the government to solve the case and come clean.

‹•›

Mr. Samuel Duah came to see me at about ten o'clock on Sunday morning. He came in traditional Adinkra cloth with a woman he introduced as his wife. His handshake was tight and his palm was sweaty. I could tell he was uneasy. He apologized three times for coming in the morning, saying it was the best time to escape notice as people all over town were finding their way to their churches. Then Mr. Duah said that both Asare's office and his home had been ransacked by soldiers.

Luckily a contact had tipped him off a day earlier, and this had helped him to destroy some of the sensitive information about Asare and his business.

"I need your help, Charlotte. I can't hang on to Asare's documents. I will be next on their list to search and these documents are too important to destroy," said Samuel Duah.

"I've only known Asare for a few months," I protested.

"Charlotte, it's because you are just an acquaintance that you're our best bet."

"No. This may be dangerous," I said.

"Take a look at the package. There is no contraband, no drugs, and nothing stolen. Just some contracts, bank details and some money. Asare stands to lose everything he has worked for if these things get into the wrong hands. You will be safe. Nobody in Kumasi associates you with Asare."

"Okay," I whispered. In spite of his mild demeanor, Samuel Duah was a very persuasive man.

"Asare is a good man. He would do anything for you. He will repay your kindness many times over."

"I know."

"When the heat blows over in a couple of weeks, I shall return for the package. I know Asare will be grateful to you for the rest of his life."

He turned to his wife, who quickly opened her bag and whipped out a bulky package. Mr. Duah passed it to me.

"We shouldn't stay for very long. If anyone asks about us, just tell them an aunt and uncle of yours are visiting Kumasi for a funeral. Let's be discreet, shall we?" said Mr. Duah, still whispering.

I nodded.

"Don't worry, things will soon blow over. Asare said you were both clever and courageous, and I believe you are."

They left, and I didn't see them off downstairs. I checked to make sure my curtains were drawn together, and then I opened the package.

There was a brown envelope that held papers, but there was another envelope that held wads and wads of money. Much of it was in hundred-dollar notes, but there were some pounds sterling and cedi notes, too.

I wondered how much money I had in my possession. How could they trust me with so much?

Then I wondered what I had gotten myself into. I should have said no. But now it was too late.

‹•›

Mary came charging into the room. "Turn the radio on. Turn it on!" she shouted.

Radio 2 broke the news that the half-burnt bodies of the kidnapped judges and the army officer had been discovered in a bush fifty kilometers from Accra. Rainfall on the night of the capture had doused the petrol fire set by the murderers.

The site of discovery, near a military range, pointed dramatically to the military as the perpetrators of the crime. The news was still fragmentary, but nothing could mask the chilling brazenness of the act. Everyone agreed that it could only have been authorized in high places.

I listened at the top of each hour for new details, making notes for our next meeting.

I remembered a conversation I had overheard between my father and one of my uncles who was a lecturer at the University of Ghana. It was after the 1979 coup which had seen the Ghanaian brain drain at its worst, as senior lecturers, civil servants, lawyers, judges and businessmen fled from persecution. That fear had dissipated as the AFRC handed power back to the civilians after three and a half months. Now the unspoken fear was that Rawlings and his comrades had used the intervening time to perfect a more gory vision.

I remembered my uncle had made reference to the horrendous violence of the Khmer Rouge in Cambodia. Now, one could no longer discount those fears as baseless.

‹•›

The Ghana Bar Association staged a protest march in Accra. They demanded a broad investigation and punishment for everyone connected with the murders. Fingers were still pointed at people associated with the government. Rawlings was implicated as the vehicle used to arrest the judges was traced to his house.

Banahene was angry that Ghanaians were not causing enough of a disturbance about the kidnapping and murder of the judges.

"People should have been protesting day and night. If it has happened to somebody, it could happen to anybody. Someone has to stand up to this government. I cannot stand the many complaints our parents make in their bedrooms, only to come out and live life as usual," he said.

"But they don't have any power against a state that might just show up and kidnap them from their homes in the middle of the night," I said.

"And if we don't speak up, they may take us one by one until there is nobody left to protest," he insisted.

It was only then that I told Banahene about the man in the Pajero. How he had almost run me down on my way back from the library and later threatened me.

Banahene was shocked. "Why didn't you tell me? Everyone knows that Pajeros are the most popular unmarked military cars."

"We were all so indignant about the judges that I just forgot," I said.

Then I told him about Mr. Samuel Duah and the package he had deposited in my keep.

This was too much for Banahene.

"I don't get it, Charlotte. Why would you take such risks for Asare, especially at this time? I just don't get it," he muttered over and over.

I tried to reassure him. "It's only because he was a good friend. I know he is in need, so I can't abandon him."

I watched Banahene struggle, and I wondered if our relationship would stand up to these stresses. I began to feel desperate as I failed to convince him of my motive. I didn't want our relationship to end. I couldn't let that happen.

"Banahene, you know I love you. You also know I have given up Asare. It's just that these times are so crazy, and Asare really needs my help," I pleaded.

"I don't like it, Charlotte. Sometimes I wonder what would have happened if he'd come back and pursued you. And I wonder why you haven't told me all this while that you're in touch with Asare and members of his family," said Banahene.

"I guess I didn't want to scare you off," I admitted.

"Well, I'm scared for you now," he said, staring steadily at me. "I don't know what to make of all this, Charlotte. Who was in the Pajero? And why did they feel the need to scare you? Why not me, or Jordan? Is it because you are associated with Asare?"

"I don't think the Pajero has anything to do with Asare. They are probably hoping that I will scare easily because I am a woman," I said.

"What about that student who asked you about your

sugar daddy on manifesto night? There was something deliberate about him, and I haven't seen him since."

"I thought you said he was just a student playing dirty," I said.

"Still, he was very calculating. Everybody knows about Mary's Mr. Opoku, but I was surprised that a stranger would know about you and Asare. What else do they know about you?"

"That hurts, Banahene."

He looked away from me as I touched his shoulder, pleading.

"I really am sorry, Charlotte. I'm concerned that someone may be setting you up for a fall. You must get rid of Asare's items. You can't trust anybody these days."

"The money is a lot, perhaps twenty thousand dollars. I can't just throw it away. I can't ask Mr. Opoku to keep it, because everyone knows he's Asare's friend. I could ask Juaben, but then, Sylvia is her roommate," I said.

"Sylvia could be part of your problem. She knows you well enough but is affiliated with the other side. You must be careful about her," said Banahene.

"Do you think Sylvia would give information about me to others?"

"She was your friend and not mine," he replied.

Although Banahene walked me down the path, he said little. The truth had come at a cost, and the chill between us made me wonder what else was in store for me.

17

When Mr. Opoku came to visit, he confirmed that soldiers had ransacked Asare's house in Kumasi. They seized his BMW and took away his papers. They trampled his garden and broke the gate. They made a mess of everything.

"Ah! These people! Why can't they leave the man alone?" Mr. Opoku exclaimed. He was still shaken and had come to Mary for comfort.

"Nobody's safe these days," said Mary.

I thought of Asare's beautiful house and garden. I remembered riding in the olive-green Witch, which purred like a satisfied cat. It was so sad that Asare could be so poorly treated even in his absence. I wondered who he would turn to for comfort.

"What is it about Asare that bothers the revolution?" I asked. In the previous AFRC government, many wealthy businessmen were charged with corruption and jailed. Others had their bank accounts frozen and their assets seized.

"If they could pin anything on him, they would have done so already. Ɛyɛ anibere ne abrɔ — envy and malice!" said Mary.

"Asare is sometimes too direct when he is telling people off. Some years ago he angered one of the key people in the new government. I think that man has a grudge. Soldiers have been to his offices several times to harass his workers. This time they went to his house, too," said Mr. Opoku.

"He can't come back now — not after the killing of the judges," said Mary.

"Do you know Mr. Samuel Duah?" I asked Mr. Opoku.

"Yes, he's a good guy — Asare's cousin. How do you know him?"

"He brought me something from Asare."

"A letter?"

"Yes."

"Have you replied?" he asked.

I hesitated. For some reason, I didn't want to talk about the money and the papers.

"It's like that, eh? Out of sight, out of mind? Women!" said Mr. Opoku.

"That's not fair," said Mary.

"I know. I'm just sorry about everything that's happened. The coup, Asare's business, his home, even his girl — all gone. Life can be hard. Boys abrɛ paa!"

Mr. Opoku seemed to wilt in the armchair, his lower lip caught between his teeth. We sat quietly for a while. I think we were all grieving for Asare, and that first carefree term that I had spent at Tech. How quickly things had changed.

173

⟨•⟩

Days passed, and Mary wanted to know where Banahene was. I told her that course work was keeping him away from Africa Hall. We had spent so much time campaigning that we now had to focus on our studies. It was a convenient excuse and Mary was convinced, but Juaben had a question in her eyes.

I was spending more time with Juaben because Sylvia was hardly ever in the hall. She was always busy with Mensah, but I sometimes bumped into her at our English lectures. Although we were friendlier with each other since the SRC elections, I understood that we would never go back to former times.

I thought about Asare's package every day when I felt for it among my clothes. There was no way I could take that kind of money home when term ended. I would have to ask Mary to hide it for me.

⟨•⟩

On Thursday, I came back from lectures and found that Banahene had left a note in my pigeon hole.

"Urgent meeting 7 p.m. tomorrow, Friday, at the SRC office."

I was glad for any communication from him, even if it was just about business. My heart did that wobble thing. How I missed him!

Friday evening was cool because it had rained earlier in the day. Once upon a time I would have been dressing for a party or a night out, but things had changed. I dressed up nicely for the meeting, even using eye makeup and a touch of lipstick.

Jordan and Banahene were in the office when I got there. I took my seat next to Jordan on the other side of the desk. The lone bulb shone bleakly in the room.

"I'm only going to record what is safe to record," I said.

Banahene nodded. He opened an envelope and read an invitation from the NUGS secretariat to meet with our counterparts in the other universities. We were going to discuss strategies to pressure the government to return the country to a democratic process.

"It goes without saying that we will soon be going on aluta," said Jordan.

Banahene agreed. Peaceful but noisy public demonstrations were the tried and true process for students, ever since our universities had been in existence. But governments hated aluta.

I thought about our vice chancellor. I would have to send him a memo informing him of any student action that we would plan to take.

⟨•⟩

The NUGS executive released a statement to the press. It was a brief note condemning the kidnapping and killing of the judges. NUGS also made a plea for justice, and then they called on the PNDC to hand over power to a democratic government.

As leaders of our local SRC, our part was to present the NUGS position to the students. Next we would oversee a motion to protest against the government. We went into organization mode, and I typed out the memos calling for an emergency general meeting.

The Great Hall was as full as it had been on manifesto night. I watched from the stage as students streamed in to find their seats. It was hard to settle them. We hadn't had such a turnout for a long while.

We did start at last, and Banahene did a good job of explaining the agenda for the meeting. Every mention of the judges brought loud expressions of student anger and shouts of "Down with the PNDC."

I unfolded the details of the case so far. Everything hinged on the car that was used to pick up the judges. It was a Fiat Campagnola — a not-very-common military-style off-road vehicle. The distraught husband of the female judge had seen it and noted its number. In an unusually bold move a reporter had linked the car to one of those often parked at Rawlings' house.

It didn't take much more to get a student to table a motion asking for justice and a return to democracy. Another vote passed overwhelmingly in favor of a demonstration. Somebody started singing, "We shall overcome." Everyone joined in. My excitement was mixed with fear.

"Don't worry, Charlotte. Right now the government is embarrassed about the killing of the judges, and I think they won't want to be seen as violent," Jordan said.

I hoped he was right. But if the killing of the judges was just the beginning of bloodshed, then our acts of defiance could trigger a deluge of violence. Our students agreed that silence was a poor option. Together we would put an end to evil before it gained strength.

‹•›

It had been a moody day. It wasn't hot but it was humid, and the sun had struggled all day with the clouds. If I was superstitious, I would have said that there was a quarrel going on among the gods.

At 4 p.m. students converged on Paa Joe Stadium from every direction. We were not there to witness an exciting game of varsity hockey. We were gathering to pray. A call had gone out from the executive of the Inter-Hall Christian Fellowship to all its members in every residence.

From the floodlit field, the praise leader and his band led us in song. The voices around me grew louder, and there were spontaneous outbursts of talking in tongues. I focused my mind on God and prayed for one thing only — safety.

Jordan had invited Banahene and me to the prayer meeting. Juaben met us there and we stood side by side with hundreds of students in the stands. Mary was there, too, and I was glad for the presence of my friends.

Two masterful preachers read from the Bible, and many voices broke into a tumult of prayer. As I stood with hands raised, my faith rose to believe in the words of affirmation. The president of the fellowship was persuaded that we had been called into student leadership for such a time.

We all prayed for safety. We prayed for our civil rights to be upheld and for all negative and evil plans of the government to fail. We prayed against the advance of godless socialism and military rule. And we prayed against the manifestation of violence during our upcoming protest.

I joined in with all the other voices to shout Amen!

‹•›

Early the next morning students gathered on the road just behind Africa Hall. They came dressed in T-shirts and sweatpants or jeans. The loudest students were holding placards. Others had their messages scrawled in ink on their shirts. DEMOCRACY NOW! WE WANT THE TRUTH! GO AWAY MURDERERS! GHANA SHALL BE FREE! PEACE FOR GHANA! JUSTICE FOR THE JUDGES!

I watched as perhaps a thousand of us lined up in ranks. I wondered why people were so cheerful on a day like this.

Then, megaphone in hand, Banahene addressed the crowd. This was his aluta as president of the SRC.

"Students of UST, thank you for coming out to make a stand for this country. This is a peaceful protest. We will march until we get to the Circle at Kejetia. We will stay in our ranks and sing our songs. We will not be distracted or get caught up in fights. We will not harm people or wreck any property, including cars. Even if people insult us or throw things at us, we shall keep our calm. We shall hand our letter over to the regional secretary and then we shall make our speeches and return home. Please stay with the group, everyone. Be safe!"

One of the cheer leaders raised the traditional militant Asafo chant, "Osee yee." And we sang it with one voice. I couldn't help thinking this is what it would have sounded like in centuries past when Ashanti went to war.

Then a thousand pairs of feet began to move.

"Come on, Charlotte," said Jordan. He took my hand. The powerful tread of feet moving in one direction was terrifying. I could almost believe that we would change the world.

We sang and my heart pounded with adrenaline. But still the questions came to mind. What would happen if someone fell and got trampled to death beneath our feet? What if soldiers suddenly appeared and shot at us? The ensuing panic would no doubt end in a stampede. I was doubly glad we had spent the time praying, even though you wouldn't know it from the chants of defiance that we sang to keep us going. This time I didn't mind the profanity of the substituted lyrics.

We awakened the town of Kumasi from suburb to suburb until we arrived at Kejetia market, pumped, sweaty and proud. All along the sides of the road, the townsfolk gathered to gawk or cheer. A few shouted insults at us.

It had taken two hours to get to the center of town. Banahene delivered his speech again by megaphone. He spoke about the kidnapping and murder of the judges and the government's complicity. He addressed the students but he spoke for the benefit of the townspeople. We sang several songs and crowned our efforts with a mighty osee yee, fit for the King of Ashanti. It was Jordan who led the chant. For a skinny man, he had the voice of a giant. And after the rousing war chant had died down, he passed the megaphone to me.

I don't know what seized me but I threw all caution to the wind. I found myself yelling defiance at the government. I broke into a rendition of "We Shall Overcome," screaming into the megaphone. The crowd seemed larger than before. A man pushed his way through to those who surrounded me. He identified himself as a reporter with the *Spectator* and asked for an interview. And the crowd tightened around us when he produced his tape recorder.

"Can you state your name clearly and tell me what the students are doing here today," he said.

I was by then exuberantly beyond care and couldn't wait to announce our position.

"The students of UST are here today on behalf of Mother Ghana. We will not stop demonstrating until the government is returned to the people. We are demonstrating against the poor state of human rights in this great country, the murders of three judges and an army officer, and against the restrictive budget of this government. We want a return to democracy. Power to the people! A luta continua!" I shouted.

18

Some people hailed taxis for the return journey to campus. I might have done the same if I could have gotten away with it, but as good leaders we had to walk the entire journey back. So we sang, cheered on by wayside admirers. Those who had brought money bought oranges, bananas and groundnuts. They shared freely with others. We must have boosted the wayside trade by at least a hundred percent.

Our songs dried up along the way. We arrived on campus exhausted.

Mary had stayed behind. I was sorry that she had missed out on such a historic event.

"I just don't like the craziness of public demonstrations. Anything could have happened," she said.

"But Mary, we were so united and so powerful together. It was beautiful," I said.

I couldn't believe that we had done this without damage to civilian property, and without clashing with the police.

God was truly on our side.

ALUTA

<•>

A group of ladies were talking in the foyer at breakfast time. They gave me a loud cheer when they saw me. I just waved back, too shy to take the credit for what we had all achieved.

"Charlotte, you are strong-o," said Mr. Afriyie from the porter's lodge. Then he showed me the newspaper he was reading. There, plastered over the front page, was a picture of me with my fist in a power salute and a megaphone to my mouth. And the reporter had published my name alongside the brief interview I gave.

My excitement lasted for just a moment. Suddenly, I realized that all over the country, people would be reading this piece. I could imagine Dad's face when he saw mine on the first page of the paper. He would shout for my mother, wag his finger prophetically and say, "Tell your daughter Charlotte to be very, very careful — wɔn hwɛ yie paa!

Once more, I was glad for the distance between Kumasi and Accra.

<•>

Although we were very involved in student affairs together, my hope was fading for a more intimate relationship with Banahene. I couldn't help thinking how paradoxical it was that the more we worked together, the less we connected emotionally.

It didn't make sense that I was losing Banahene. How could Asare affect us so deeply when he was so far away?

I was lying on my bed just thinking those thoughts when I heard the shouting. Then Mary came running from the fifth floor, where she had been visiting with her mates. Everyone was standing out on the landing, looking over the balustrade.

A bus had parked on the road behind Block A, exactly where we had started out on aluta just two days before. We saw men with sticks climbing out of the bus and walking towards our hall.

"Miners," said Mary, just as I recognized the words Obuasi Gold Mine painted on the side of the bus. "What are they here for?"

The miners seemed a little unsure of what to do, as they milled around the hall entrance.

I shouted down to the men below, "What do you want?"

"Shut up over there, you mouf-mouf girl. We'll teach you sense," said one man in a red hat, waving a stick.

And just like that we were perched on the brink of panic.

From the eighth floor, I shouted to my hall mates, "Those of you who play hockey, go and get your hockey sticks! We may have to defend ourselves."

The girls began to shout at the men. Down below, the men with sticks also got much rowdier. I feared that they might soon charge indoors, but the porter had sneaked up to the door and locked it.

Still, they could easily climb up our latticed wall onto the top of the lower roof. From there it was easy to reach the first floor. This was what we did when we came back to a locked hall after hours of partying. I feared for any girl who might be walking back to the hall, so we kept a lookout and shouted people away long before they got to the danger zone.

All that shouting must have worked, because all of a sudden we heard chanting, and then I saw boys jogging down our driveway holding sticks, hockey sticks and stones. I saw Banahene in the charge.

The battle was one of shouts and threats. And the enemy, seeing scores of excited young men charging down the driveway, retreated swiftly to their bus. It was all over in minutes, as the Obuasi Mine bus screeched away at top speed, while our men hurled stones after them.

We went downstairs and pressed the porters to open the doors to the boys. We met them with triumphant cheers and draped our admiration all over them. In the foyer there were hugs and kisses for the chivalrous Republic Hall fighters.

"Thanks, guys," I said, giving a few of them high fives.

Then I got to Banahene. For a few moments I just looked at him, hoping he could see my heartfelt thanks. I didn't hug him.

"Is this it, or will they be back?" I asked.

"I don't know," said Banahene, still breathless from excitement.

"It was too easy," I said.

"I agree. Tonight we'll set a guard near Africa Hall. Tell the girls to collect stones and sticks just in case the attackers return."

The day began to feel much brighter as the distance eased between Banahene and me. Laughter came easily as we talked about recent events. And we took the longer route to Republic Hall.

"It's time to publish an open letter to Ghanaian workers about their Workers' Defence Committees. They don't realize they're just tools of manipulation by the government," I said.

"None of the big papers would publish our letters. They are all state owned," said Banahene.

"What about the smaller privately owned papers? People read them, too."

"It would take more than one letter to make a dent in public perception. Workers have been taught to hate students who come with their freshly earned degrees to earn higher salaries overnight."

"I don't think they love to hate us. We must get our voices heard," I said.

"Make these suggestions when we go to Accra for the NUGS meeting. Perhaps we could come up with a great campaign for the nation," said Banahene.

"Why are we having the meeting in Accra? Is it safer?"

"It's more central," said Banahene.

We kept walking, and along the way he took my hand.

"Charlotte, I'm sorry for my behavior this past week. Can you forgive me?"

"I forgive you," I said, and I gave his fingers a tight squeeze. Like him, I didn't want to say much more about it.

‹•›

The night passed peacefully. And I soon learned that it didn't matter that the miners had lost the battle, because the state apparatus still had control of the newspapers. Mr. Afriyie showed me his newspaper and I read how we had been punished by the miners until we begged for mercy. I laughed about it with Mary and Juaben, but it irked that they had the power to make their lies stick.

After that, our rooms became small armories of stones and sticks. I placed two stones beneath Mary's bunk, and a hockey stick on the balcony. Mr. Opoku brought us two batons, which we slid beneath the bookshelf.

"This government is proving very clever. Some of their members were student leaders back when General Acheampong released soldiers against us," said Mr. Opoku. "They know they'll lose favor if soldiers attack students, so they used the miners to simulate a grassroots response."

"We have nothing to fear if they don't use soldiers. Blow for blow, we can stand up to anyone, unless guns are brought in," I said.

Banahene was more cautious. "I think they'll use soldiers if they have to. They are showing some restraint because Ghanaians are appalled at them for the killing of the judges. They have to show tolerance while they deny their part in the murders. But trust me, they are ruthless."

Still, the fact that they had not used soldiers to attack us gave me some confidence. In Ghana, there was nothing really to fear except soldiers with guns.

In the next few days we returned to our routines, only more watchful than ever before. The next day we heard that students at the University of Ghana, Legon, had demonstrated. They were chased out of the university by workers organized by the WDC. Banahene feared that the universities could be summarily closed.

‹•›

Someone pinned a note on the hall notice board: *Degrees Are Forever.*

Exams were drawing nigh, and in the midst of all these happenings we still had papers to submit. Banahene and I were making up for lost time so we took to studying together. Because he had a single room, that meant we had our privacy.

My whole world seemed to revolve around Banahene and the SRC, and Mary often complained about my absence from our room.

Republic Hall was a rowdy place, but when it came time to study in the evenings, the noise died down.

I had worked for two hours one night and was tired, so I lay down to rest a while. I even dozed off. When I awakened, I checked my watch. It was quite late.

"Stay. What's the point of going back to Africa Hall when the porter would likely not answer you at the door? You take the bed. I have papers to write anyway," said Banahene.

I drew the covers over me and closed my eyes. I had become so tender in my heart. Sure, I had rested on Banahene's bed before and even snoozed for an hour or so, but this felt different. I closed my eyes and slept.

I awakened later as I felt him close by. He was sitting on the bed and I knew he had been staring at me. He kissed me and brought my body slowly to life. I kissed him back.

We began to touch each other and raise fires that were hard to snuff out. It was all the excitement and the anxiety of almost losing each other. We just kept going until we made love. It was my first time.

I felt I had crossed a threshold from which neither of us could return. I tried not to think that I had done anything wrong. We needed healing, and I was so in love.

⟨•⟩

On Tuesday Banahene brought newspapers to the SRC office. The front pages were full of pictures of law students demonstrating in Accra. Apparently they had come into direct conflict with police, and a few of the students were hurt by flailing police batons. Thank God nobody had been shot.

"What will happen when the Cape Coast students demonstrate in the next few days? Let's hope Sharon and her mates fare better than the Legon students," said Banahene.

"Maybe they will send fishermen after them," said Jordan, chuckling. And I imagined hundreds of them being chased into the sea by angry Fanti fishermen wielding paddles and nets.

We discussed the meeting that NUGS was convening in Accra. A recent communiqué was marked Confidential, and it had the meeting date and place. All student councils were expected to attend.

There were things I wanted to share at the meeting. I also wanted to reconnect with Sharon. Jordan felt it would be too important a meeting to miss, and so we decided we would all go.

Everything was to be done in confidence. I couldn't even tell Mary or Juaben about it. Jordan feared that we might easily be recognized in a team, and so he insisted that we travel to Accra on different buses.

I would be the first to board an STC bus for Accra. Banahene would board a private bus, and Jordan would hitch a ride with a friend from Kumasi town. We planned to connect on the day of the meeting at the address we had been given in Madina.

"Don't carry the address with you. Memorize it and destroy the memo," said Banahene.

"Is it really that dangerous?" I asked.

"This is what the NUGS president told me to do," said Banahene.

"This sounds like Mission Impossible. This message is about to self-destruct," I said, but nobody laughed.

⟨•⟩

We left Jordan at Queen's Hall after the meeting, and our plan was to study in Banahene's room. But last night's memories were on my mind, making it hard to concentrate. Then Banahene said it was time to eat. I watched as he mixed lightly soaked gari and corned beef together in a bowl with shitor and ketchup. Then we ate with naked fingers from the same bowl, and Earl Klugh's music in the background.

Afterwards we washed our dishes together, pouring water on each other's hands. Then we talked. We remembered how we had fallen in love in the cool shadow of the Kwahu Hills. We remembered the fearsome boneshaker rides and laughed. We kissed.

Banahene teased my blouse off my shoulders, and then his shirt followed. My skirt was riding high about my waist.

I felt the intrusion of guilt but I muffled it as Banahene's lips seized mine in a passionate kiss. His caresses were urgent, on my face and my neck and down my shoulder — a blazing trail. And bit by bit my desire matched his until at last we came, our legs intertwined in a strange embrace.

19

Dawn was a kaleidoscope of sounds — a cock crowing close by and the sound of cars driving away in the distance. I lay there for some moments until I remembered I was at home in Accra. Instead of my narrow bunkbed in Room 803, I had spent the night alone in a queen-sized bed with a ceiling fan whirring far above me. My sister Sarah was away at boarding school.

My journey to Accra had gone smoothly, and my dreams had been full of love. I lay there for half an hour, thinking about Banahene. Actually I was worried, because now that we'd had sex twice, I wondered what would make us stop. I had never thought of contraceptives before, and I balked at the idea of entering deeply into a sexual relationship while I was unmarried and still in school. It didn't feel right to just keep going even if one was prepared for it. I'd have to broach the subject with him once we returned to school.

I waited until I heard my dad's car start. He was always early to school, but I knew he would have a lecture planned for me sometime after work.

Outside, the day was moist and gray. To help my mother, I fed the chickens in their coop. Then I washed quickly and dressed up in a brown skirt and a red checked blouse. I borrowed my mother's low-heeled brown sandals and joined her for breakfast for the dining room. I loved my mother's rice-water, and I was happy for warm teabread with a bit of melted Blue Band margarine. I hadn't realized how much I had missed home.

Mama took the morning off from work. She wanted to spend some time with me as I was leaving the next day for school. I told her I had missed home and her cooking. I especially needed a bottle of her shrimp-rich shitor to last for the rest of the term.

"Any excuse is a good one if it brings you home, Charlotte. We saw your photograph in the newspaper. Your father was very concerned. These soldiers are bad. You shouldn't go and play in their yard. Just the other day, Mr. Samson who lives near the golf course was driving home from work. You know the traffic at Circle at five o'clock, and how everyone needs a lot of patience to get around it. Well, some soldiers forced their way through the traffic and scraped his car. When he complained, they bundled him into their Pajero and got one soldier to drive his car away. Do you know that they shaved his head with a broken bottle, cutting him all over his scalp? And he has never found his car since. Charlotte, be careful with these people. You have no idea what they are capable of doing."

"Yes, Mama," I said. "I am very careful these days. I'll make sure I'm not in the news again. That was silly of me."

I told Mama that I was going to town to deliver a message to Juaben's parents. It was a necessary lie. I couldn't very well tell her I was attending a secret NUGS meeting.

"Don't be too long," she said.

Outside, the sun had come out and the dew had long since disappeared. I flagged down a taxi at the junction. It was ten o'clock, and our meeting was scheduled for eleven. I would take two more taxis just to get to my destination. It was safer to travel this way — hustling from point to point.

We were to meet at a home in Madina, a nondescript place tucked away from the public eye. I had memorized the directions and destroyed the memo. There was a little knot of anxiety in my belly. Someone had said that courage existed not because of the lack of fear, but by the actions one takes in spite of fear.

Slowly, the taxi driver edged the car into the flow of traffic and I settled down for the trip.

Up ahead, a solitary soldier flagged us down. Drop-in taxis were frowned upon in the revolution, and taxi sharing was common. He opened the back door and sat down, slamming the door shut. The taxi driver started the car again.

"Gondar Barracks," ordered the soldier behind us.

Normally, all taxis were registered only for particular routes. Soldiers were the exception to all rules so I knew our driver would have to change direction. Still, it was unusual for an officer to commandeer a vehicle with others in it.

I wasn't going to argue with him, and so I asked the driver to kindly let me off at the next junction.

"Keep driving," ordered the officer as the driver slowed the car down. I was about to protest when he said harshly, "Charlotte Adom, we request your help with our current investigations."

My heart dropped into my belly at the sound of my name.

"What investigations? You have the wrong Charlotte Adom. I live at Achimota School. My father teaches biology," I said, hoping the taxi driver would remember my name. He was the only witness to my capture.

"Shut up!" roared the man from behind me.

"Where are you taking me, sir?"

"Drive!" shouted the officer to the driver. He never told me his name, his rank, or his unit.

The taxi driver stepped hard on the gas, and all I could think of was the name Gondar Barracks, ringing in my ears.

‹•›

The officer gave directions to the taxi driver as we went along, and it didn't seem to me that we were headed for Gondar Barracks. There were so many turns, this way and that, until I lost my bearings.

At last we entered a driveway. The taxi stopped and the soldier hustled me out of the car into a waiting white Pajero, which had two other men in it. He pushed me between them and locked the car. He went round to the front and slammed the door. Someone started the car, and we backed out so forcefully that I was sure we would hit the wall.

I began to wonder if this was what had happened to the judges. My heart raced uncontrollably and fear almost blinded me.

I started to shout in the car, "Let me out of here."

But one man reached across and slapped me. "Listen, we are only going to question you but if you make noise I shall knock you out."

Tears sprang to my eyes, but I didn't want to sob. I began to say the Lord's Prayer under my breath.

They took me to a house behind tall white walls. They shut a heavy black gate behind us. And when the car stopped at last, they took me to a room which was quite empty except for a desk and two chairs. My captor shoved me into a chair and locked the door, leaving me by myself.

I looked around me. I tried to take comfort in the fact that I wasn't tied up and this was not a barracks. Then it occurred to me that it might have been better to be in some barracks or government institution where records might be kept of my presence.

The door opened, and another man came in. He was tall and skinny. He had a tribal mark cut into one cheek, and small beady eyes that had ice in them. So far nobody had introduced themselves and neither did this man.

"Charlotte Adom? I am from National Security," he said stiffly. "Can you answer these questions?"

And with that he sat down and opened a file. And the interrogation began.

‹•›

Someone was shaking me awake. I opened my eyes with difficulty as if my eyelids were weighted with bricks.

It was the man who had kidnapped me in the taxi. He was the worst of the lot, so angry and fierce. This time there was a grin on his face that made me cringe. I could tell that something had happened.

My dream was not just a dream. I had said things. The interrogator must have mixed something with my drink. What had I said? Who had I put into trouble?

Worse, I could smell the urine which had now dried on my clothes.

"Get up," commanded the officer.

"Can I leave now?"

"You want to go where?" he demanded, and his laughter grated on my ears.

He grabbed my elbow, marched me out of the room to the next room. There was only a mattress there. And dirty shutters for windows. The windows were closed and it was dark and stuffy, even though it was still daylight.

"Wait here," he said.

He left me for hours inside the room. I heard cars start up, I heard the gate open. Sometimes I heard talk and even laughter. Once I banged on the door and a man came to the door.

"What?"

"I want to go home," I said.

"Lady, just be quiet. It's better to be quiet. They will take you home," he said.

I thought there was a trace of kindness in his voice.

"Help me, please. I want to urinate," I said.

"Wait." And he brought me a Milo tin. "Just urinate

here, lady. Don't make these people angry," he whispered. Then he locked the door again.

After I urinated in the tin, I set it in a corner of the room. Then I sat down on the dusty floor and waited. Perhaps they wanted to interrogate me again. Various scenarios rushed through my mind, and I wondered if I would be tortured or killed. I began to pray in feverish whispers.

The hours passed. Then the door to the small room opened. Perhaps they were ready to release me at last.

My captor came in again. He came towards me, and an unfriendly smile stretched his face taut. Grasping my upper arm, he yanked me to my feet. All of a sudden he was pressing me against the wall, and his harsh breath reeked of alcohol.

Half staggering, he steered me towards the dirty mattress on the floor. It had no sheets but it had a pillow that was stained with what could have been sweat, saliva or even vomit. His big rough hands pulled at me. He fell on top of me. Big hands held me down while I struggled. My skirt was already riding up. With one hand he pushed my thighs apart and straddled me. With his other hand, he pulled my underwear down. Then with one hand against my mouth, he entered me, smothering my cries back down my throat. I gagged and added my vomit to the stained pillow.

I wondered if anyone could hear my heart thumping against my chest. The hand that had smothered me fell away from my mouth, plastered with vomit. I heard him swear. Then he smeared his hand against the wall just above my head. My mouth was free but the desire to scream had abandoned me.

It was too late. I had already died many times, and to be found now was of little benefit.

Strangely, it flashed through my mind that I would turn nineteen in another week. But for me, the world ended right then.

At last he rolled off me, pulled up his pants and staggered out of the room. Slowly I got up and adjusted my clothes as best as I could. I tried the door. To my surprise, it opened. When I got to the gate, the man who had brought me the Milo tin obliged me by opening it. He could not look at me. I kept on walking until a taxi driver honked hard behind me.

"Drop in?" he asked.

"Achimota," I replied. All I could think of was running water and soap to scrub the filth away.

⟨•⟩

I got home as the clock in the dining room struck six o'clock. I showered and went to bed. I told my mother I wasn't feeling well. I refused my dinner but I took some paracetamol with a glass of Fanta. I drifted in and out of sleep all through the night, waking up more than once with a scream in my throat. Each time I stifled it, and I tried to block the memory of what had happened to me. I woke up late the next morning, still feigning sickness. Mama wanted me to take a chloroquine treatment course but I declined.

"I think it's just exhaustion. I should be okay if I just rest," I said.

"You will have all the time to rest, it seems," said Mama.

She brought both the *Daily Graphic* and the *Times* with headlines screaming: *Universities Closed by Order, PNDC. Universities in Accra, Kumasi and Cape Coast Closed Indefinitely.*

I thought about my passport and all Asare's money given to me for safekeeping. They were in my closet at Africa Hall.

"I have to go back to school and pack out," I said to my mother.

"Wait for your father to come home," she said.

I scoured the newspapers. All the stories were about unruly students who had refused to go to lectures and who were instead demonstrating unlawfully and destroying public property.

Another article described the confessions of student activists from all three universities. The confessions included the spreading of lies and misinformation, leading to sabotage and subversion of the government. Someone confessed to smoking marijuana, and another to cocaine dealing. I knew that those students had been beaten or tortured to write those confessions. Who knew what else could have happened to them? It seemed like they had been on to us all even before the meeting at Madina. There was no word from Banahene or Jordan, and I prayed that they had escaped.

Dad came home for supper. He had already decided I was staying home.

"I'm sure your roommate will move your things to her home. Wait a while, and when things have died down you can return to Kumasi to get your things. It may be providence that brought you home safely," he said.

This time it was easy to obey my dad's instruction to lie low and stay home. I swallowed my pain. I buried my memories, and I would never have spoken of my ordeal because the shame was too great.

‹•›

I became obsessed with washing. I wanted to believe that nothing had happened to me — that nothing had changed, but I had a strange suspicion that everyone could see what I had endured. As the days passed, I helped Mama around the house and tried to be normal.

Two weeks later, Jordan came to visit. He had missed the Madina meeting because his friend's car had broken down on the way to Accra. They had spent two days on the road.

He said that Banahene had left the country the very day we were scheduled to meet. His parents had sent him away, driving west through La Côte d'Ivoire. They had learned that his life was in danger. We could only hope to hear from him once he was safe.

Jordan said the NUGS secretary had been arrested and taken to Ussher Fort. He had been released after three days. Two other student leaders from Legon and Cape Coast had been taken to Gondar Barracks. They'd come out subdued, with heads shorn, after promising to be supportive of the government and the good people of Ghana. Sharon was safe in England. Because she was writing an exam, she had stayed in Cape Coast during the NUGS meeting. Jordan told me he would leave the country, too, if he got a chance.

20

My sister came home for the holidays and soon started vacation classes. My nights were filled with strange dreams and my days with the effort of being normal. I helped in the house as much as possible, and six weeks went by before I noticed that I had missed my period. I increased my exercise, running up and down the stairs several times a day. I also chewed kola nut and drank Coca-Cola whenever I could. A long time ago someone had told me that the sugar and the fizz were enough to reset delayed menses.

I started skipping. I did jumping jacks and pushups, all in an attempt to shake the pregnancy loose from inside me. I had the scientific picture of pregnancy in mind from my dad's textbooks of human biology. If the pregnancy was on my skin, I would have dug it out with a fingernail.

Secondary schools opened again but the universities were still closed. Accra became very hot, and weeks passed on end with no rain. Dad said even the skies were protesting the government's wrongdoing. The drought had

201

brought famine, and famine had brought a new term — Rawlings Chain, referring to the knobbly bits of rib bones that showed through starved and tightly stretched skin.

We were sitting around the dining table eating my mother's strange pawpaw stew, when all of a sudden Mama looked at me. She did not say a word until dinner was over.

After dinner I cleaned the kitchen, and then I went to my room.

After a while she knocked on my door.

"Charlotte, are you pregnant?" she demanded.

Shock was what made me admit it instantly.

"How far?" My mother's voice was low, scraping the belly.

"Three months."

"And by whom?"

I wanted to say something, but the words just would not come out of my mouth. Not even when my father was involved in the questioning, could I tell the story.

How would they believe that I really did not know if it was the soldier, or Banahene? And my pain at Dad's disappointment made me hold out like a dam.

‹•›

Dad would not look at me directly. And I stayed in my room all day unless I was commanded to come down to eat. I was not sulking, nor was I crying. I was searching for something — my own soul.

Then, one evening, I suddenly understood that I was lost to everyone whom I had loved — lost even to myself, for someone had stolen me away. This thing that separated me from those I loved would also separate my child from me.

Mama brought up the idea to send me to the Catholic convent at Kwahu-Tafo. There I could be well hidden until I delivered the child safely and quietly. Nobody would have to know apart from us, so long as the universities remained closed. Mama said if the universities reopened before the baby was born, we would figure out what to do.

I awakened before five o'clock and lay there listening to the sounds of dawn. A bird was tweeting incessantly just outside my window. I heard the first cock crow, and after that the other cocks struggled to catch up with protests of their own. A late mosquito sang in my ear, and I brushed it away. It floated on, too drunk on my blood to move any faster. I got up, followed it and smashed it against the wall, smearing the wall with blood.

Outside, someone was sweeping the yard. Then I heard footsteps in the kitchen. Mama would be cooking koko or rice-water for breakfast.

I looked at my suitcase. There were few clothes in it — mostly Mama's. She also handed me a prayer book and her rosary.

A few hours later, Dad, Mama and I sat in our Peugeot 404 on the road to Kwahu-Tafo. I watched the bush pass by, interrupted by the usual look-alike roadside villages. A few months ago, I had traveled this way to salvage cocoa from the bush. Everything was the same, and yet life would never be the same again.

‹•›

I embraced the quietness of the convent. It had to be peace I felt around me, if not inside. It was there on the thin mattress and the narrow bed. It was there in my work at the nursery where babies were nurtured, and in the garden where I was asked to grow some corn. Peace was also the daily Mass, and I rediscovered my rosary and the comfort of prayers muttered through quiet lips. And it was at the convent that I finally admitted in the confidence of the confessional that I had been raped by an unknown soldier. Even then I could not bring myself to confess that I had also been intimate with Banahene. That would be our secret, God's and mine.

Time slipped away like sand in the hand. And Christmas came — dry and cheerless as the dusty harmattan winds that blew from the north.

Mama forwarded Mary's letter to me along with a card. It had been sent care of my dad at Achimota School. It was just a note confirming that she had all my things. She had underlined *all*, and I knew what she meant — Asare's package. She also said she was going to have a church wedding on the eighth of January — a Saturday. She wanted me to come.

She had no idea how a simple note like that, carrying her warm affection, could literally save my life.

Suddenly I felt loved. I started a letter to Mary and it grew longer and longer every day until I was sure I would not post it. I had till April to wait out my pregnancy, far from the eyes of anyone I knew. But I had Mary's distant ear and in my letter I told her all those things I couldn't tell God. Mary was my lifeline. Even from afar, perhaps she could save me.

> *Dear Mary,*
> *I am pregnant and the shame of my family. I am waiting in a strange town to deliver this child, if only I survive. I am burdened not only in my womb but in my mind and soul. I have been looking for God but it is hard to see His face. In my dream, it is Banahene's face I see, before the monster appears and eats him up. Then your letter came and rays of light entered my dream. Perhaps, I can have this child and live ...*

‹•›

I woke up with abdominal pain on Sunday, the twentieth of February. At first I thought it was that old pain I had fought on the day of the coup d'état. I told the Mother of the convent that I just needed to vomit to feel better, but she disagreed. She said it was labor pain.

The baby was coming prematurely at thirty-two weeks, and I was filled with anxiety.

The midwife came and I labored through the afternoon. I lay there in awe of the new depths of pain that washed over me in waves. From a haze of sweat I heard the encouragement of the sisters as I lay with legs wide apart, grunting and pushing.

Then came the crowning, and a different kind of pain superimposed itself on the former. I welcomed it all as the baby was born. I screamed from the anguish. I was glad for the blood and the waters that escaped — glad for the cleansing after the baby came.

And for the first time, tears trickled down my face for this baby whose conception lay somewhere between violence and love.

She was conceived as a child of the revolution, lost already at the point of her birth. I held her once and searched her face, looking for signs that she was Banahene's. Finding nothing of him, I gave her to the nuns, never having put her to my breast to feed on her own milk. In my memory was the breastfeeding judge who had been kidnapped and killed one eerie night in June. Her baby, too, had lost her milk forever.

The nuns named her Esi because she was born on Sunday. They called her Nyamekye because even unwanted babies belong to God. I would always remember her face, an imprint of wetness on my memory.

Epilogue

My belly feels like pounded yam fufu with stretch marks radiating from a sunken belly button. It tells me I may never forget the one who rested there for months and months.

The nuns have blessed me. The priest has absolved me, and I am told that I am free to get on with my life. But life is some distance away in a gray fog that I have come to know so well.

I pack my things. I leave a letter in my locker along with a small donation.

Dear Mother,
Thank you for caring for me for all those months. Please call my daughter Esi N. Gana, because her father is this bleeding land.

The convent Mother waits for me in the van. We don't speak as she drives up the dusty road and turns into the transport yard. She stays with me until I have bought my ticket. Still she waits until I climb on the bus. Then she watches while the bus starts. She waves as we drive out of the gates.

I am gone out of their lives, having given them something of mine to hold.

On the STC bus, we are sitting six on a row meant for five people. The radio is blaring.

Ghana has become Rawlings' country. He has done his worst but he is still lord. The people have weathered drought, famine and gas shortages, but they are still singing highlife songs.

I hear the talking drums, a signal for the news on GBC radio. It is noon hour and the bus is hot, even though the windows are open to the stirred-up wind.

The first thing I hear is "The Secretary for Education, Dr. Ampem, has announced that the universities will open in two weeks. On March 25, all students are to report to their places of matriculation."

There is a burst of chatter on the bus. I look around. I wonder if there are university students on this bus. It is hard to tell because everybody looks worn out, and not at all like those people with whom I lived on Tech campus — daring, young, energetic and free — young people lusting to know their own voice and mind, and thinking they can change the world. Maybe I look tired, too.

I am thinking of Africa Hall. I'm thinking of Mary and Juaben. I'm wondering if the others think I have joined the refugees to Europe and America. I'm wondering what excuses my mother has made to all those who may have asked of me. What has she told my sister?

I'm thinking of Banahene and wondering if he has looked for me. Would he send me a letter care of my dad at the school? I'm wondering if Jordan has left the country, and if all those who left will return once more.

The radio announcer's voice becomes nothing more than a rumble scratched with static. Until suddenly I hear a name: "The Edmund Asare Bediako trial continues today."

I strain to hear what is being said.

"Asare Bediako, a Ghanaian businessman with concerns in petroleum and natural gas, is facing the second day of his trial in an Accra Fast Track court. He is charged with treason for conspiring to overthrow the government, and if found guilty can face execution."

I'm crying soundlessly. I'm weeping without tears. I'm grieving for Asare. I'm mourning for us all.

The journey is long and the ride bumpy. Sound fades and so do the faces all around me. I know this feeling. There is a fog coming my way. Usually I fight it, but this time I enter willingly.

I'm on a plane climbing high above the clouds. When I look down I see a huge crowd. It is Mary's wedding. She's dressed in a flowing white robe with a tiara and a veil. Juaben, Sylvia and Sharon are her bridesmaids and they're all wearing red. Derek, Jordan and Mensah are the groomsmen, smartly dressed in identical black suits. But I can't find Banahene or Asare anywhere.

I see Mr. Opoku standing at the back of the crowd. I wonder who Mary is getting married to. There he stands, tall and arrogant in ceremonial military clothes with a sword at his side.

I know then that I must stop the wedding. I must stop Mary before she makes her vows.

"Wait! Stop," I shout.

ALUTA

But nobody can hear me. My plane keeps climbing and everything fades away except the fog, the melody of the bridal march and faint cries of *A luta continua, vitória é certa.*

Author's Note

Ghana was the first country in Sub-Saharan Africa to gain its independence from Britain in 1957. Since then there have been several coups d'état staged by groups in the military. These coups have been characterized by social upheaval, loss of life and property. Many have blamed the difficulties in Ghana over the years to the instability caused by coups and poor government.

On June 4, 1979, the third coup d'état brought Flight Lieutenant Jerry John Rawlings and the Armed Forces Revolutionary Council to power. The life of this government was three and a half months, and its goal was to accomplish a so-called House Cleaning exercise. This led to an unprecedented number of executions, including the killing of three former military heads of state and other senior military officers of the past government without due process. It was also a period of martial law and grave persecution of former members of government, business leaders, petty merchants and ordinary individuals who were accused of corruption.

Rawlings and the AFRC handed over power to a democratically elected government only to have it overthrown by Rawlings in just twenty-seven months. On December

211

ALUTA

31, 1981, Rawlings came to power for the second time and founded the Provisional National Defence Council — PNDC.

Aluta is a work of fiction set in the early years of PNDC rule, during which Rawlings appeared to favor socialism for a season. During this period there were many human rights abuses against civilians, military officers and even student leaders.

There is a long tradition of student activism in Ghana's politics. Large protest marches (alutas) have been organized over the years by the National Union of Ghana Students, which includes all students of tertiary institutions, and Student Representative Councils, which are local to each college. Student activism has sometimes brought the change that Ghanaians desire.

J.J. Rawlings was the dictator of Ghana until December 1992 — ten years. Then democratic elections returned him to power as the president of the Fourth Republic for the next eight years. For almost twenty years Ghana was in one way or other Rawlings' country until 2000, when the New Patriotic Party won the elections with J. A. Kufuor as president.

Since 2000 Ghana has become a more stable democracy, having undergone another change of government without violence. It has also become a place of greater civil freedoms and human rights. Like many other developing countries, Ghana continues to struggle with issues of corruption, poverty and mismanagement. However, Ghanaians take their freedoms seriously and continue to press for better governance.

Glossary

Abrɛ paa: Very tired.

Adinkra: Akan symbols.

Adinkrahene: Adinkra symbol representing the supreme God.

AFRC: Armed Forces Revolutionary Council.

Ahenemma: A style of native sandals first worn by royalty.

Akan: Large language group comprising several tribal nations (48 percent of Ghanaians).

Apɔnkye-kakra: Light soup cooked with goat meat.

Apotɔyewa: Clay mortar for crushing vegetables.

Asafo: Militia.

Ashanti: Akan-speaking nation in Ghana.

Awɔɔshia: Sleepover.

Bangla (slang): University student's food allowance.

Banku: Fermented corn and cassava dumpling.

Batakari: Cotton smock.

Cedi: Ghanaian currency.

Dɛn asɛm ni: What kind of trouble is this?

Dɔ-me-a-bra: Come if you love me.

Dwɛɛ: Cocky.

Ɛyɛ anibere ne abrɔ: It is envy and malice.

Fanti: Akan-speaking nation in Ghana.

Fufu: A ball of cooked and pounded plantain, cassava or yam.

Ga: Language group in Ghana.

213

Gari: Roasted granules of cassava.

Gondar Barracks: Army barracks in Accra.

Highlife: Contemporary West African dance music.

Hwɛ yie: Be careful.

Jheri curl: Curly perm.

Jollof: Pilau.

Kalabule: Illegal hiking of prices.

Kelewele: Spicy fried plantain.

Kenkey: Fermented corn dumpling wrapped in leaves.

Koko: Cornmeal porridge.

Kola: Caffeine-containing nut.

Me mpɛ me ho asɛm: I don't want trouble.

Mouf-mouf: Mouthy.

Nkɔdaa: Children.

Nkwaseasɛm: Nonsense.

NUGS: National Union of Ghana Students.

Oburoni: Caucasian/fair one.

Okro: Vegetable seed pod used in sauces and soups.

Oyiwa: There it is/I told you so.

PNDC: Provisional National Defence Council.

PNP: People's National Party.

Political suit: Mao suit with short sleeves, made popular by Ghana's first president.

Rice-water: Rice porridge.

Shiee: Expression of wonder.

Shitor: Spicy fried pepper sauce.

Sikyi: Recreational Ashanti dance.

SRC: Student Representative Council.

STC: State Transport Corporation.

Tweaa: Expletive for disgust.

Twi: Language of the Akan people.

UST: University of Science and Technology, Kumasi.

Waakye: Purplish-brown dish of rice and beans.